Random Thoughts:

A Writer's Notebook

Mark Nelson O'Brien

WeBe Books Publishing
c/o Authentic Endeavors Publishing
Clarks Summit, PA 18411

Random Thoughts: A Writer's Notebook
ISBN: 978-1-955668-42-2 (Paperback)
       978-1-955668-43-9 (Hardback)
       978-1-955668-44-6 (eBook)
Library of Congress Control Number: 2022918244

Table of Contents

Table of Contents

Table of Contents

Face the Music

My employment history started with my first electric guitar.

Sometime in early 1968, my father took me to Azzolina's Music Box, a store, now long gone, on Colony Street in Meriden, Connecticut. For $200, we bought a guitar and a little amp, both made by a Japanese company called Univox. To say they were not of high quality would be kind. We didn't know that then. And it didn't matter. In my 14-year-old mind, I was already one of the Beatles. Creedence Clearwater Revival, Jimi Hendrix, Mountain, B.B. King, Johnny Winter, Cream, and my myriad other favorite bands and guitar heroes hadn't even found me yet.

My father made it clear that the guitar and the amp weren't gifts: I'd have to pay him back the $200 somehow. My first choice, somehow — God, apparently, hadn't invented child-labor laws yet — was to go to work in the tobacco fields during that summer. It was a bad choice for four reasons:

First, the temperatures reached 120 degrees and more under the airless nets that covered the fields.

Second, since tobacco leaves aren't picked until late in the summer, the early part of the season is spent on one's butt, shimmying down the rows of plants in the moist dirt, picking suckers from the bottoms of the stalks. Suckers are small leaves that would otherwise siphon off the moisture and nutrients from the soil, preventing them from reaching the broad leaves of the plant. We called the process suckering.

Third, sitting in that dampness all day produced the same itching one incurs from sitting in a wet bathing suit on the vinyl upholstery of your dad's car on the way home from the beach.

Fourth, the juice from the plants that got on one's hands and clothing was well-nigh impossible to get off — ever.

Since I only lasted two weeks, we don't even have to call that my first job.

In the fall of that same year, my freshman year in high school — and since I still owed my father almost all of the $200 he'd spotted me for the guitar and the amp — I bought a paper route. Plan A was that I'd work the route with my brother, Keith. Plan B turned out to be working the route by myself.

At that time, Meriden had two newspapers, both published by the same company. The Morning Record was published ... well ... in the morning. The Meriden Journal was published in the afternoon. I delivered *The Morning Record.*

I don't remember how many customers I had. I do remember the route was big enough that my papers had to be dropped for me in two bundles. One was dropped at the end of our driveway. The other was dropped at the far south end of Bradley Avenue, at the corner of Bradley and Hancock Street. I'd have to untie the bundles, put the papers into my bag, folds up for ease of delivery.

Since Bradley Avenue was a wide boulevard, I'd work my way south, delivering papers to my customers on the west side of the boulevard and on all the side streets that ran west from it. After picking up the bundle at the corner of Bradley and Hancock, I'd work my way back north up Bradley, delivering papers to my customers on the east side of the boulevard and on all the side streets that ran east from it.

I'd set my alarm for 5:00 a.m., six days a week (the Record wasn't published on Sundays), and be out of the house before the first glimmer of sunrise. For all the time I had the route, I never once believed I was actually getting up that early.

I detested that job in the winter. As a result of its being bitterly cold and dark, I'd have to dress appropriately. That meant wearing gloves. That made handling the papers more difficult. The bad news was it made delivering the papers much more time-consuming. The good news was I got to work on my vocabulary, honing my penchant for profanity to a razor's edge and turning the dark morning air blue on many the occasion.

But some of my favorite memories, to this day, are of working that route in the summer. I loved rainy summer mornings especially. I'd go out wearing just a pair of shorts. No shirt. No shoes. And I'd run the entire route. I felt like Tarzan — free, unbound, nothing between me and Nature. I was very aware of my youth and fitness. And since I was on the track team at my high school, the running was effortless, the bag felt weightless, and the rain was as cleansing and purifying as it was in all the myths I hadn't even read yet.

I kept the paper route for two years. When I turned 16, in my junior year of high school, I got my first real job. I waited the counter and flipped burgers at McDonald's on West Main Street for $1.60 an hour.

I'm now dozens of guitars beyond that cheap Univox. And I've played through more amps than can possibly be good for anyone. We are, for better or worse, the sum of our stories.

I never missed the tobacco field. But on some summer mornings, I still miss that paper route.

©Mark Nelson O'Brien

Chapman Beach: Part One

In the summer of 1964, my parents rented a small, red cottage on Cherry Street at Chapman Beach in Westbrook, Connecticut, for seven weeks, at 75 dollars a week. Those were, indeed, the days. They rented the same cottage for the entire summer in 1965. And in 1967, they rented a different cottage in Chapman Beach. Those were the best summers of my life.

Headed east along the shoreline from Chapman Beach, the next beach is Chalker Beach. The one after that is Indian Town. That matters because that same summer, my cousin, Gary, was staying in a cottage in Indian Town. That meant Gary and I, both 10 years old that summer, were within walking distance up the beach from each other. It also meant Gary and I could share comic books with each other. (In case you're curious, they were 12 cents apiece in those glorious days.)

I primarily read the flagship titles of DC Comics: Superman and Batman. But Gary had discovered the Marvel Comics world. His sharing it with me changed mine. (Gary still doesn't believe any of this.) As a result, *Origins of Marvel Comics* and *Son of Origins of Marvel Comics*, both of which I was fortunate enough to acquire before they went out of print and became collectors' items, are two of my most treasured possessions. I frequently re-read them — not just to experience the stories again — but to remember what I am and why.

It's true: I'm a writer because of Stan Lee. And it's that simple. I knew, even at 10, that his Marvel stories had what my DC stories did not: personality. They had an authentic voice. They had actual life. They had wry wit and sarcastic bravado. They were revealing and human. They used language — even more than imagery, a fantastic and audacious feat in a predominantly visual medium — to engage, move, entertain, and inspire me. They had style. I knew it because I felt it. Yes. My calling found me at 10.

What Stan Lee gave me most of all was the courage to imagine. I was no longer afraid of I don't know. Rather, I was encouraged and energized by I don't know yet. Yet transforms I don't know into positive potential. It connotes the possibility that what there is to know, or what needs to be known, hasn't been created yet. It yields the opportunity to create it. And that opportunity yields an equation something like this:

Opportunity x imagination = the number of possibilities.

Is anything more inspiring, more empowering, or more liberating than that? The numbers are all — and always — in our favor.

Ang Lee's film, *Hulk*, debuted on June 20, 2003, the 17th birthday of my younger son, Quinn. We saw the film together. When we got home that evening, I sent an email to Stan Lee, telling him the story I just told you, telling him we'd seen the film, and asking him how rewarding it was that — 40 years after the fact — cinematic technology had finally caught up to his imagination.

He didn't reply. It didn't matter. He'd given me more than enough 39 summers before.

©1974 by Marvel Comics Group

©1975 by Marvel Comics Group

Chapman Beach: Part Two

Since I mentioned staying in Westbrook, Connecticut, in Chapman Beach: Part One — and since I lived in Westbrook from 2006 to 2015 — this story recounts a more recent encounter, prompted by my having read the news item below:

WESTBROOK, CONN — The Westbrook Fire Marshall is trying to determine the cause of an early morning fire at 20 Cherry St. Fire crews got the fire under control in 35 minutes. Most of the damage was done to the second floor. The cause is under investigation. No one was home at the time of the fire. No firefighters were injured while fighting the fire.

The tiny, red cottage my family had rented in the summers of 1964 and 1965 was on Cherry Street. Since those are the happiest, most memorable summers of my life, the story clicked, made me wonder, then passed in the rush of work and life until

…

At the end of a training ride for Bike MS: Cape Cod Getaway, as I pedaled west on Route 1, the Boston Post Road, I approached Chapman Beach. Recalling the news item, I turned in to satisfy my curiosity. I passed cottages unchanged and memories undimmed for 50 years. I passed new cottages and new faces, reminding me change is as constant as the un-frayed fabric of our lives. I turned left on Cherry Street.

In the lot on which the cottage in which I spent those wondrous summers once stood was a vacant, newly bulldozed scar, bearing charred remnants of the fire a month earlier. I stopped for a hushed, frozen moment, recalling the old red cottage more vividly than I now saw its fragmentary remains. I wanted to cry … but not there. I wanted to mourn the cottage and the boyhood that were no more … but not then. I heard voices.

I looked to my right. Across the street and on the other side of a hedgerow sat two elderly gentlemen. In lawn chairs, they sat at a glass-top table, shaded by an umbrella, sharing a drink and a conversation much like all the others they'd been sharing for more years than I've been alive — Joe, an Italian gentleman, and Pat, an Irishman. I pushed my bike across the street.

Over the hedge, I asked if the Warnes family still owned the old cottage. I asked if the Hirsts still lived next door and if the descendants of Old Man Spencer, the lobsterman, still lived out back aside the creek. I asked if children still netted blue crabs in that creek. They looked at me as if I were an apparition from their own pasts, rather than a nostalgic, middle-aged man, trying to recapture some of his own.

Joe said, "Young man, you know too much. You better come over here and sit down." I pushed my bike through a break in the hedge, introduced myself, removed my helmet and my gloves, shook their hands, and sat down. Joe asked if I wanted a glass of water. I thanked him and declined. He said, "I'd offer you something else. But it's too expensive."

Then he asked, "Did you know Vic Verdolini?" The Verdolini family had owned a cottage on Chapman Beach Road. I replied, "Yes. He was a Meriden native like me. Vic went to school with my Mom and Dad. His restaurant on Hanover Street made my favorite pizza. And I went to school with Vic's kids, Gary and Lisa." Joe looked at Pat and said, "This guy might be for real."

I asked the gentlemen if they knew the Mottrams, who owned the cottage at the end of Cherry Street. They did. I asked them if they knew the Bransfields, who owned the cottage around the block. They did. I asked them if they remembered a beautiful girl named Cathy Marotta from a cottage on Fox Lane. They did. I asked if they remembered the Lawtons, who rented the blue cottage by the beach. They did. I asked if they remembered what the name had been on the front of that cottage. Pat said, "Harvard. And the one right behind it was Little Harvard." He was right.

Joe said, "You have a pretty good memory." I assured him it was selective. I recalled every moment — every ray of sun, every fresh smell, and every brush of soft sea air from those long-ago summers. I remembered going to the row of mailboxes on Cherry Street one day in 1965 to get the Meriden newspaper, which was forwarded to us during the summer. I remembered seeing a photograph of Gerry Levy, a Meriden neighbor, a schoolmate of my older sister, and an Army medic in Vietnam. The photo showed him emerging from the jungle with a wounded G.I. over his shoulder. I remember another day the same newspaper carried the story of Gerry's death. And I remember finding Gerry's name on the Vietnam Veterans Memorial in Washington when I visited there in the early '90s. In contrast, just the week before, I'd forgotten to bring my wallet when taking a client to lunch.

Joe replied, "Ah ... you're still a kid." I told him I had a little too much gray hair to qualify as a kid. He pointed to his shining scalp and said, "At least you still got yours."

At that point, Pat chimed in: "I'll bet I was out of school before you were born." I said I doubted that. He said, "I wasn't able to finish college till I got out of the service after the second World War. I graduated in 1946." Joe saw my eyes widen and added, "I'm 87. He's 93."

All I could say in response was, "God bless both of you."

With that, Joe looked at Pat: "Well, should we take a walk to the beach?" Pat bounced up and said, "It's about time." I took my cue, stood, shook their hands again, and thanked them for a wonderful conversation. Joe pointed at my bike and said, "The next time you come around here on that thing, you better stop and say hello." I told him I was finally old enough and smart enough not to make promises. But for him, I'd make an exception.

We parted company. Joe and Pat went their way talking and laughing. I went mine with tears in my eyes and goose bumps from a profound sense of connectedness.

Life does, indeed, go on. The threads of mine are unbreakable.

Chapman Beach   Westbrook, Conn.

Alive on Arrival

I read a story once called, "What Not to Do in a Morgue", about a British gentleman's attempt to earn some travel money. It was intended to be funny. But as you might surmise, morgue humor is no laughing matter.

I know. During my first two years out of high school, I was responsible for a morgue. Specifically, I was a house orderly at the now-defunct Meriden-Wallingford hospital in my hometown of Meriden, Connecticut.

I had a number of morgue-related duties: I had to transport bodies to the morgue — from the patient floors, from the emergency room, from ambulances arriving with DOAs. I had to assist during autopsies for some reason, keeping pathologists company while they took bodies apart searching for or confirming causes of death. I had to help morticians transport bodies from the morgue to their hearses (a task for which they tipped me, always leaving me feeling mercenarily ghoulish).

Sometimes I had to sew up the empty thoracic and abdominal cavities of the bodies if the morticians happened to be particularly meticulous about keeping their body bags and hearses clean.

And I saw much: To help determine if the cause of death was suicide, I had to help the State Police measure the arm of a man — from his shoulder to the second knuckle of his index finger — as well as the shotgun — from barrel-end to trigger — that had blown out his chest. I had to remove the neoprene rope from the neck of an attorney who'd climbed atop a file cabinet and stepped off into eternity. I had to pull hard-hat shards from the head of a man who'd been in a trench that hadn't been buttressed with shoring boxes. His skull was as flat as Wile E. Coyote's after being the victim of his own Acme Anvil.

I was once compelled by the State Medical Examiner to weigh the body of a nine-year-old girl whose head had been run over by a school bus. I saw the disintegrated remains of a man who thought standing in front of a train bound from Hartford to New Haven was preferable to carrying on.

For obvious reasons, that job made me wonder two things every day:

What in the world made the people who hired me imagine a boy in his late teens — having taken no aptitude tests, let alone being given preparation or training — was psychologically or emotionally equipped to contend with some of the job's more grim tasks?

Aside from teaching me I wasn't cut out for a career in medicine, what in the world could I take from the job that might be of lasting value or meaning for the rest of my life?

Almost 50 years later, question #1 remains elusively unanswerable. But question #2 answered itself on some transcendent occasions. Here are two:

First, a woman in her 80s, a Mrs. Ruland, whose late husband had been a physician of sufficient renown to have had a clinic named for him at the Masonic Home and Hospital in Wallingford, Connecticut (now Masonicare), was a patient in one of the surgery units. She'd been admitted to have her left eye removed. Every morning of her stay, before and after her surgery, eye patch and all, she got out of bed, made the bed, and dressed herself in her own clothes.

Until the day she was discharged, I spent as much time as I could spare in her room sitting, talking, and learning from that gentle, gracious lady.

Second, I was asked (and allowed for reasons I never understood) to give a gentleman suffering from some intestinal malady a soap suds enema. This consisted of filling an IV bag with warm water, dumping a few packets of Castile soap into the water, hanging the IV bag well above the patient, inserting a clamped tube descending from the bag into his rectum, removing the clamp from the tube, and letting gravity do the rest.

The patient suffered from cerebral palsy. He was barely ambulatory but managed to get around with two aluminum canes with aluminum cuffs through which he slipped both hands before grabbing the handles of the canes. After taking the entirety of the IV bag's contents into his colon — and the painfully pressured agitation that water and soap must have caused him — he could have easily evacuated into the bed pan I'd brought into his room. He wouldn't have it.

That man possessed so much fortitude, so much modesty, and so much dignity, he insisted on my handing him his canes so he could walk all the way across the room to the bathroom. When he came out, he asked me why I was crying. Not many of us get to witness that kind of strength and courage.

Perhaps informed by my experience in the hospital, question #2 above continues to yield profound lessons. Among them:

Life is short, sometimes brutally so. That tends to make every moment precious and every additional day a treasure.

Loss is universal. But sorrow allows us to witness transcendent grace, the wisdom of acceptance, and the strength to endure.

We control nothing. Knowing that gives us the freedom to celebrate every occasion of joy and to triumph over the shortness of life, to overcome loss and sorrow, and to be free from all illusions of control.

We're all alive on arrival. What we do after we get here is up to us.

©2014 by Meriden Record-Journal

©2014 by Meriden Record-Journal

What I Learned From Boss Pig

I have a confession: I play Angry Birds 2.

I started playing to keep myself occupied while waiting for people to respond to instant messages (which, much like the Express Lanes in grocery-store checkouts, are anything but instant), waiting in line at the DMV, waiting for doctor or dentist appointments, waiting at railroad crossings, or keeping my wife, Anne, company on the couch while she watches *Fixer to Fabulous*, *Property Brothers*, *Love It or Li$t It*, *Windy City Rehab*, *Home Town*, *Good Bones*, *Flip or Flop*, *House Hunters Renovation*, *This Old House*, *Grand Designs*, and *Dr. Pimple Popper*.

But after playing for a while (say, roughly 350 levels or so) something revelatory and quite unexpected happened: In the face of what seemed like insurmountable frustration at having to replay every room in every level, sometimes innumerably, only to be unable to reach — or to be unable to conquer — the Boss Pig (or the King Pig, or the Chef Pig, or the Foreman Pig, or any other of his myriad manifestations), I learned patience.

First, Angry Birds 2 taught me the patience to study. The game can be a series of mindlessly distracting tactical moves (which attracted my initial interest), or it can be a strategic, fully engaging, and relentless pursuit of a singular goal (which attracts my abiding interest): Blast the Boss Pig to Hell, move on to other levels and, in some instances, to other worlds entirely. Wow!

Second, Angry Birds 2 taught me to persist, to endure, to recognize the temporary nature of frustration, and to realize the conquering power of tenacity. By its addictive nature (or mine), the game compels players to keep coming back, regardless of the seemingly impossible adversity — to think, to examine, to analyze, and to find a way to move on.

To find a way to move on. Think about that. Moving on, determining to move on, finding a way to move on, settling for nothing less than moving on is the modus operandi for a rewarding life. It's the remedy for procrastination. It's the antidote for anxiety. It's the defeat of paralyzing depression. It's the answer to the age-old philosophical question:

Why are we here?

To move on. Period

Finally, Angry Birds 2 is of a piece with two other things that have always helped me move on. The first is a quote from Mikal Gilmore, from his book, Shot in the Heart. I read the book in the late '90s, during a bout of depression characterized by stark, unrelenting terror.

The book recounts the Gilmore family's dark history, leading to the execution of Mikal's older brother, Gary, in 1977, by a Utah firing squad. (Gary's last words: "Let's do it.") The book's unremitting bleakness had me wondering at every turn of the page why I continued to read it while experiencing my own period of darkness. It felt masochistic.

But there, on page 374, I found my answer.

Gilmore wrote: "Depression is a hard experience to communicate, and perhaps a hard one to understand, but once you've had it you don't forget it. It makes you look on the rest of the world with a bit more compassion, and it also causes you to watch the corners of your life more closely, so you can spot the darkness rapidly if it begins to creep back in."

Reading that gave me no instant relief. But I was in the care of a psychiatrist, and I was surrounded by friends who'd also experienced depression. They told me I wasn't myself — but I would be again. They were right. And Gilmore's words assured me they were right.

Even more, Gilmore's words eventually led me to see the depression I'd experienced as a gift. It taught me the temporary nature of misery. It taught me much about what I can and cannot control. It helped me to understand my capacity to overcome affliction and misfortune. It did make me more compassionate. It did teach me to watch the corners of my life ever more acutely. And it helped me to realize all I was capable of achieving if I mustered the resolve and the energy to just ... move ... on.

The other thing that never loses its ability to help me move on is this quote from the brilliant inventor, accomplished businessman, technological pioneer, and ardent player of Angry Birds, Thomas Edison: "Many of life's failures are people who did not realize how close they were to success when they gave up."

Give up? Not a chance. Giving up is a Boss Pig in a poke.

Now if you'll excuse me, I have to get back in the game.

©2015 Rovio Entertainment

That's Faith

When he was in his early teens, I took my younger son, Quinn, along with his friend and teammate, Kevin, to play in a weekend AAU basketball tournament in Albany, New York. After the games, as we wound our way out of town on a chilly, overcast Sunday afternoon, we saw a Starbucks. I pulled in. The boys opted to wait in the car. I took their drink orders and went inside.

As I took my place in line, about five people deep in the queue, I noticed the woman directly in front of me. She had thick, wavy, dark brown hair, barely streaked with strands of white. She wore a cardigan that matched the brown of her hair. As she turned to greet me, I saw the left side of her sweater was depressed in the front. Just above that depression, she wore a button that said, "Breast cancer: Say it. Fight it. Damn it."

Her eyes were radiant. Her smile was luminous. She said, "Well, hello!" as if her only reason for being there was to greet me.

In her amazing presence, all I could do was ask: "Why do I have the feeling you're so much more alive than I am?"

Love is only what we come to live,
The waking, breathing, and all we give,
A crystal passing, reflected in our eyes,
Eclipsing all the jealously and lies.
(Mountain, "For Yasgur's Farm")

She proceeded to tell me, unabashed and without artifice, about her cancer diagnosis, about the support of her husband and her children, about the professionalism and compassion of her medical team, and about her belief in God. Then she pointed at her hair and said, "God even gave me this. Before chemo, my hair was thin and straight. Now it's thick and wavy. That's a gift."

Our conversation continued as the line inched forward. She told me her name was Lisa May. She'd driven from Long Island to bring her son to the same tournament in which mine played. Within the field of her energy, I felt like a battery being re-charged, like a sponge absorbing light. We talked for another 10 minutes or so. Then her coffee was up. She took it, said goodbye, and left.

A moment later, with my coffee and the drinks for the boys in hand, I headed out the door. To my right as I angled toward my car was a slight embankment. Atop it was a strip mall like the one Starbucks was in. I saw Lisa getting into her car up there. Putting our drinks on the roof of my car, I asked the boys to stay put for another minute. Then I ran up to catch Lisa before she left.

If you hear the song I sing,
You will understand.
You hold the key to love and fear
All in your trembling hand.
Just one key unlocks them both.
It's there at your command.
(Lizz Wright, "Get Together")

I approached her and said, a little haltingly: "Do you know how things happen sometimes, and you get the distinct sense they're supposed to happen?"

She smiled and said, "Yes."

"I was supposed to meet you today, Lisa May. I don't need to know the reason. I just need to know there is one."

Still smiling, Lisa said only: "That's faith."

I would not have been surprised at all if she'd sprouted wings and flown away.

©2014 NBC News

The Big Why

In New England, where I happen to live, there's a regional supermarket chain called Big Y. Years ago, a graphic designer and I wanted to pitch an ad campaign to Big Y featuring a cartoon figure of Socrates. We wanted to call the campaign The Big Why. We never made the pitch.

The Big Why, indeed.

I met the graphic designer, whose name was Jeff, in 1985. We became fast friends — rapt conversationalists, fellow concert-goers, and drinking buddies. He was amazingly talented and brilliantly creative. He was married to a woman equally talented and creative. They were partners in their design business, which did extremely well. They owned a beautiful home with a separate but attached building that served as their studio.

If there was one person I've ever known about whom I'd have said, "He's got it made," it was Jeff. I could never tell if it was his talent, his easy laugh, his bright eyes, his unfailing smile, his financial success, or all of those things that gave me that conviction. Maybe it was the fact that he was as close to Peter Pan as might be humanly possible. He was fiercely determined to not grow up or old. He was always looking for the next mountain to climb, the next stream to fish, the next party to attend, the next opportunity to live and to live his life to the fullest and happiest.

In the mid-'90s, Jeff and his wife left the east coast. I lost touch with them. I wasn't surprised. Jeff wasn't one for looking back geographically, chronologically, or emotionally. He'd cross my mind on occasion. But I imagined he'd re-surface at some point when it served one of his life's purposes.

Several years ago, I awoke on a Saturday morning with an odd compulsion to find Jeff or to at least find out what he was up to. I went on the Web and started searching. I learned he'd committed suicide in 2005.

The Big Why, indeed.

I don't know if you've been asked it yet, but it's become popular in marketing, self-help, holistic-healing, pseudo-psychological, pointless-rhetoric, and talk-at-the-expense-of-action circles to ask people, "What's your why?" All of that is attributable to a young British chap named Simon Sinek, who's managed to turn our cataclysmic dearth of self-faith and common sense — and our limitless capacity for pathological gullibility — into a gold mine, beginning with the publication of his first book ten years ago, Start With Why. God bless him for being enterprising. Shame on us for making him a rich celebrity.

Relatedly, I had a conversation the other night with a woman to whom I was recently connected on LinkedIn. She asked if I knew of Simon, then she asked, "Why do you write? What is your why? Can you tell me in five words?"

I said, "I avoid Simon Sinek and his ilk in the same way I avoid Oprah, Ebola, live hand grenades, kale, Real Housewives, cement mixers with brake failure, raking leaves, taking a beating, and rotten eggs. I write to restore self-faith."

If we were to restore our self-faith and common sense, people like Jeff would still be alive. People like Simon Sinek would still be poor and unknown. People like us would be content, productive, and self-sufficient. We'd think for ourselves and trust our own judgement. We'd live our lives in pursuit of things more creative and more rewarding than validation from others. We'd read Sheldon Kopp's book — If You Meet the Buddha on the Road, Kill Him — and look to ourselves for the truths we seek. We'd read Emerson and take every word to heart:

To believe your own thought, to believe that what is true for you in your private heart is true for all men — that is genius ... A man should learn to detect and watch that gleam of light which flashes across his mind from within ... Yet he dismisses without notice his thought, because it is his. In every work of genius we recognize our own rejected thoughts: they come back to us with a certain alienated majesty. Great works of art have no more affecting lesson for us than this. They teach us to abide by our spontaneous impression with good-humored inflexibility — then most when the whole cry of voices is on the other side. Else, to-morrow a stranger will say with masterly good sense precisely what we have thought and felt all the time, and we shall be forced to take with shame our own opinion from another. ... Trust thyself: every heart vibrates to that iron string. (Ralph Waldo Emerson, "Self-Reliance")

I'll always be amazed by and distressed at our lack of self-faith. I'll always be saddened by people like Jeff who take their own lives. I'll always be disdainful of people like Simon who exploit our weakness. I'll always be curious about why common sense is so inscrutably uncommon. I'll always marvel at our predilections for doubt, for second-guessing, for questioning ourselves, and for ignoring the singular genius in each of us:

genius: noun — attendant spirit present from one's birth (Oxford English Dictionary)

We all have that genius. We all have the capacity to manifest and fulfill it. We all have the facilities for wonder, for joy, for soul-reward, for expressing — by whatever our respective means — precisely what we have thought and felt all the time. And by that expression, we all have the potential to change the world, one genius at a time.

Until we accept that truth, I'll be writing.

The Big Why, indeed.

image courtesy of Vecteezy

A Matter of Letters

On a Monday afternoon in 1991, I'd left the office in which I worked in downtown Hartford, Connecticut, to get a cup of coffee. Over the weekend immediately prior, I'd seen the Terry Gilliam film, *The Fisher King*, starring Robin Williams and Jeff Bridges. While the coherence of the film left much to be desired, the resonance of its mythological references and archetypes had greatly affected me. (I'm very much a devotee of Joseph Campbell and his book, *The Hero with a Thousand Faces*.) On Monday, I was still haunted by much of what I'd seen.

As I crossed Main Street from Central Row and State House Square, angling north across Pearl Street and up Main toward Asylum Street, a homeless person approached me. He was a young man, mid-30s perhaps, dressed in dirty, dark blue twill work pants and an equally dirty and tattered blue plaid flannel shirt. He hadn't shaved for a week or more. His hair was unkempt and stringy. His eyes were steely blue. And they never left mine.

As he approached, clearly intending to accost me, I prepared myself for one of the typical stories: My car broke down. I need gas money. I need train fare. I need money for food. I need to feed my family. I wasn't sure what he would say. But I was positive it wouldn't be the truth. He stood in front of me and stopped. Though there was room to walk past him, I stopped, too.

Still looking me square in the eye — with something in them that looked like serenity, rather than the angst, agitation, and desperation I was expecting — he said: "I'm trying to find the difference between should and shouldn't. I think it's a matter of letters."

He didn't ask me for anything. I'd never given so much as a penny to a street person. I gave that young man a five-dollar bill without thinking twice or taking my eyes off of his. I felt as if I were looking into the eyes of the Robin Williams character in The Fisher King. And I thanked him.

I had no idea how I could go back to work. I couldn't even imagine walking into the coffee shop and being composed enough to order a cup. So, I did neither. I turned south on Main Street and wandered aimlessly but thoughtfully for an hour or so.

I certainly couldn't explain to anyone what had just happened. How? To whom? If you don't believe in life-altering moments and your life is altered in a moment, how do you explain that? Answer: You don't. You just accept it and adjust.

I had no idea who he was. I didn't know his story. I couldn't know what misfortune had befallen him or why he was on the street. I couldn't presume to judge him. Most important, I couldn't imagine what it felt like to be without family and friends, without shelter, without clean clothes, without a shower and toiletries, unable to be sure when and from where my next meal would come — to be without the dignity and self-possession of all of that.

And that young man surely had no idea who I was. He likely had no knowledge of *The Fisher King*. He couldn't have known how it affected me. He couldn't have known I'm a writer, a student of words, and a lover of language. He couldn't have known a subtly profound play on words would freeze me in my tracks, rivet my attention, and alter me profoundly. He couldn't possibly have known any of that, could he?

Maybe this is a better question: Could it possibly be accidental that, of all the people that young man might have approached that day, I would be the one to be blown away — to be changed in an instant — by a turn of phrase so clever as to qualify as some kind of linguistic philosophy?

No.

There are no accidents. There are only signs. Sometimes those signs are people. It's our job to be awake enough to heed those signs, those messengers, to learn lessons from them, to make responsible decisions based on those lessons, and to live our lives according to what they teach us.

I'm trying to find the difference between life and light. I think it's a matter of faith.

photo courtesy of Wikimedia Commons

My Father's Eyes

This story is named for the Eric Clapton song with the same title.

My father was a guy who took most things very seriously. I rarely saw him laugh at home. He was meticulous in the way he cared for our home, for our yard (in which he made my next-younger brother, Keith, and me spend hours on end working), for his cars, for his shoes and his clothes. He disciplined us severely. (When I was 6 or 7 and Keith a year-and-a-half younger, we'd gone to the doctor for our booster shots, whatever those were. We made the mistake of telling Dad our arms hurt. He made us do pushups because, "That's what we did in the Marines.") He got his Marine Corp flattop cut every two weeks at the same barbershop, by the same barber, Paul Zeiser. And when Paul retired, his son, Armand, cut my father's hair. My father never grew a mustache, never grew a beard. And he certainly wasn't much for jokes or tricks, except …

Whenever we'd hand my father a present — for Christmas, for his birthday, for Father's Day, or anything else — he'd do exactly the same things: He'd hold it and move it up and down as if weighing it with his hands, he'd pretend to be taking careful note of the size of the package, and he'd hold it up to his ear and shake it — all in the seeming effort to divine its contents. He'd do that until my older sister, my two younger brothers, and I were beside ourselves with frustration. Then he'd laugh and un-wrap the package.

And then there was his favorite: At the south end of Oregon Road in Meriden, the now-historic Red Bridge crossed the Quinnipiac River to connect Oregon Road with Cheshire Road if you turn left to head toward South Meriden — or River Road if you turn right to head toward Cheshire. (It never made any sense to us, either.) The old Red Bridge, which has now been replaced, was a steel-frame structure with wooden planking that formed the driving surface. Even then, in the 1960s, the bridge's best days were well behind it.

Without fail, as we approached the bridge in our car — with my father driving, my mother in the front seat next to him, and Keith and me in the back seat — my father would start to warm us up: "Oh, no. We have to go over the bridge. I hope we make it. I hope it doesn't fall apart before we get to the other side." Keith and I would start to sweat.

Then my father would drive across that bridge as slowly as he possibly could without actually stopping. The bridge would creak, groan, and tremble as if it were about to fall into the river and take us with it. Keith and I would be having conniptions in the back seat, fully panicked, looking for the ejector buttons, and screaming at the top of our lungs, "GO! GO!! GO!!!"

My mother would just look out the passenger-side window and shake her head.

I don't know what kinds of pressures compelled my father to bottle up his sense of humor as much as he did. But on the occasions on which he let it out, he was as mischievous as they come.

And his blue Irish eyes shone like the sun.

photo courtesy of Bridgehunters.com: Historic Bridges of the United States

I Volunteered for This

I once read an article in Inc. magazine entitled, "The Psychological Price of Entrepreneurship". The article said this, in part: "Many ... entrepreneurs ... harbor secret demons: Before they made it big, they struggled through moments of near-debilitating anxiety and despair — times when it seemed everything might crumble."

And it hit home.

I take every word of the article to be true. I accept every explanation and rationalization for every episode of depression it cites and every act of self-inflicted lethality it recounts. I relate to every effect. But I can't help noting the article stops short of identifying the cause of the depression and lethality, of which entrepreneurship is only a convenient, superficial symptom.

I know depression quite well. I'm not happy about it. I'm not proud of it. I am, however, grateful for it. And I'm very much okay now. But we need to do two things: (1) We need to stop calling everyone who starts a business an entrepreneur. (2) We need to acknowledge their agency in their own depression. I know that quite well, too.

On my 50th birthday — January 30, 2004 — I resigned from my job at the advertising agency at which I'd been employed for four years. I did it to found O'Brien Communications Group. I was terrified. Driving home that evening, I received a call from my older sister. She'd called to wish me a happy birthday. During the conversation, she told me her husband had just been diagnosed with prostate cancer. It was, I thought, a wake-up call.

My brother-in-law is a retired Naval officer, an Annapolis grad, completely squared away. I knew what he would do: He'd study his treatment options. He'd pick one. He'd find a place to get the treatment. He'd go there. He'd undergo the treatment. And he'd beat the cancer. That's exactly what he did. His circumstances made me think about my own: "Really? He's staring down the barrel of cancer. You quit your job. And you're the one who's terrified? Come on."

The relief was only temporary.

Despite the fact that things went well for my new company from the outset, I sank into a deep depression. As always, I had a network of supportive people and generous spirits around me.

I'd learned from experience that every time you reach out for help, your hand finds one to pull you up.

In this instance, there was one gentleman in particular who sowed the seeds of my recovery with words. He did it on two separate occasions. I have no idea if he realized the genius of his words. But I did. And I never forgot them.

On the first occasion, this exchange took place:

"Dude [he always called me Dude], do you remember being born?"

I said, "No."

"Do you know why you don't remember?"

I said, "No."

"Because it hurt so damn much. That's why. You just undertook a rebirth. Did you really think it wouldn't hurt this time?"

On the second occasion, he said this, with slightly less patience than he'd had the first time, which actually made me pay better attention:

"Dude. Think about it. You just jumped out of an airplane. Even if your parachute opened, did you really think it wouldn't hurt when you hit the ground?"

In his own way, he was reminding me fear is another manifestation of pain to be endured and managed. Fear is another source of energy to be channeled and applied constructively. But despite the poetic power of his imagery, his beautiful analogies notwithstanding, the one word that carried the most weight, the one that saved me, is "you".

His words made me the active agent of everything: You just undertook a rebirth. You just jumped out of an airplane. I did it. He wasn't giving me credit. He was pointing out the fact that I created my own reality.

He was being the antithesis of the disclaimer at the end of every commercial for every new drug: "Nausea, dizziness, liver disease, kidney failure, heart attacks, skin lesions, fatal infections, ringing in the ears, bad breath, whooping cough, hyperactivity, extreme lethargy, hangnails, terminal hiccups, and excessive nose hairs have happened." No, they haven't. They didn't just happen. Those are some of the possible consequences of the fact that you (or someone else) took that shit!

His words were also liberating. They made me go back outside the door, check my ego as I should have done at the outset, and walk back in. They made me realize — if I didn't do anything irretrievably, self-destructively, egotistically stupid (this is why

I will always contend Frankenstein should be required reading) — I wouldn't have to live with a noxious monster of my own making.

He made me realize if I were the agent of the first step, regardless of the unexpected pain it caused, I could be the agent of the second step and the third and every one thereafter. And he made me understand callings don't just happen any more than drug reactions just happen.

But callings are not free.

In the words of Harry Crews: "The little that I have learned about the world, and, more important, that I have learned about myself, has been absurdly expensive, but I have always thought it more than worth the price. There is no other way. The miracle of the world, the miracle of a rebirth of the senses, the miracle of an accepting heart can only be paid for with blood and bone. No other currency is acceptable."

The open question at the end of all this might be: Why did I do it — why did I face the fear and risk the depression and anxiety I endured? There are two answers. The first is, as Grandma O'Brien loved to say, "There's no sense being Irish if you can't be thick." And my skull is so thick as to be damn-near impenetrable.

The second answer is straight and not at all facetious: The only thing I was more afraid of than starting my own business at the ripe young age of 50 was the prospect of not starting my own business at 50 ... then having to wake up at 60 to ask myself, "What if ...?" Fear wasn't a good enough reason not to do it.

Founding my own business did not, does not, make me an entrepreneur. It doesn't make me better than anyone else. It only makes me a person determined to find his own way and to survive by his own wits.

The day the business opened — March 1, 2004 — there was no one standing beside me with a bazooka to my head. Nobody made me do anything. Nothing just happened. There was more fear and pain involved than I'd bargained for. Maybe I should have seen it coming. But I caused it. I created it. I was the agent of my own fear and pain. Since that's true, I'm not one for whom anyone should have felt bad or sorry.

I volunteered for this. And I'm enduringly grateful I did.

Finding My Faith

I was supposed to have been a nice, Irish Catholic boy. But things got off to a rocky start and never quite recovered.

I experienced my first two bouts of religion-related trepidation as an elementary-school student in the Wednesday-afternoon Catechism classes public-school students were required to attend. The first encounter took place during a film-strip presentation shared with us by the nun in charge of that day's festivities.* During that particular presentation (they were routine occurrences), Jesus let us know Roman Catholicism was the only true religion of God (unquote). He went on to explain, with what struck me as an unnerving degree of certainty, that the soul of anyone who was not of the Roman-Catholic persuasion would not achieve eternal salvation (unquote).

Since there was no mention of even temporary salvation, I thought immediately of my friends, the Moran brothers, Jeff and Barry, who lived in the house next to ours and who attended the

Congregational Church in town. My very next thought was of another friend, Marc Hoberman, who lived across the street. Marc was Jewish. Considering the facts that I was six or seven years old; I'd known Jeff, Barry, and Marc since I was five; and none of them, as far as I knew, had yet done anything reprehensible enough to earn eternal damnation, I wasn't convinced Jesus was to be taken at his Word on that one.

The second experience was more reprehensible and less forgivable than the first. The nun in charge of that day's spiritual enlightenment told us a story about missionary priests and nuns who'd been dispatched by the Church to some communist country that went unnamed. The missionaries, according to the story, had been taken prisoner by a welcoming committee of the communists in whatever unnamed country they happened to be in after refusing to renounce their faith. The nun explained to us that, after being restrained, the priests and nuns had their backs slashed open. The resulting wounds were stuffed with some kind of batting. The batting was soaked with some kind of accelerant. The missionaries burned to death when the batting was set afire. And the nun told us we should be prepared to pay the same price for our faith.

Following experience number two, I had night terrors for months. I'd see hordes of communist soldiers, small and vaguely Asian-looking, armed to the teeth and clad in green military fatigues with matching helmets, streaming across the brook that flowed south at the western boundary of our back yard. The whole world seemed to be on fire. But the soldiers, impervious to the flames and the heat, came in endless waves across that brook, stampeding double-time toward our house, my family, and the horrific demise they no doubt had in store for us.

I don't know what horrified me most — the fact that the presumably responsible adults in charge of my ostensible religious education wanted me to believe my friends were headed for Hell, the fact that my dying hideously at the hands of militant heathen hordes was something I should be conditioned to expect, or the fact that the religion to which I was supposed to be devoting myself somehow thought it was a good idea to subject children to any such obscenities.

In any case, I was out. I stopped subscribing to that perversity then and there. And I stopped going to Mass as soon as I was old enough for my parents to afford me that choice.

Nevertheless, I continued to harbor guilt and confusion. Then, in the fall of 1981, at age 27, I made the decision to start college, at long last. I was living in Meriden, Connecticut, and working in an appliance-distribution warehouse in North Haven, Connecticut — unloading trailers full of console TVs (remember those?), refrigerators, microwaves, dishwashers, stereo systems, radios, garbage disposals, and more. Enrolling in the University of Hartford, I took a course on Monday evenings called, Introduction to Management. It was like eating sawdust. On Thursday evenings, I took a course called, Introduction to Literature. It changed my plans.

The professor who taught Introduction to Literature, Bill Stull, said to me after class one evening, "I'm teaching an Honors Seminar in the spring. You should be in it." It changed my life.

"Thank you," I said sincerely if naïvely.

"I don't think you're understanding me," he said.

I asked, "What do you mean?"

He said, "The class meets three days a week, in the afternoons."

As I did the math, I realized I couldn't live in Meriden, work in North Haven, and be in Hartford three afternoons a week unless I made some changes. I did. I quit my job, moved to Hartford, and enrolled full-time.

The Honors Seminar Bill was teaching that semester was called, *The Anxious Voyage*. The syllabus for the seminar described it as a survey of quest literature. That meant we'd read a series of 20th-century novels to determine the extent to which they conformed to or manifested what Joseph Campbell called the monomyth (a term he borrowed from James Joyce). As a precursor to reading those novels, we'd read Campbell's book, *The Hero With a Thousand Faces.* That changed everything.

Monomyth refers to the fact that the lives of all of us conform to one pattern, which Campbell refers to as the hero's journey. From birth, the hero separates from the places and circumstances of his origins, journeys into darkness (physical or psychological), undergoes some form of initiation, and returns to his origins bearing the gifts of strength, knowledge, and wisdom.

My first thought as a conflicted, recovering Catholic was. "Uh oh." I imagined having to see Jesus as just one more iteration of a universal pattern would further weaken my ostensible faith, would exacerbate the doubts and questions I'd harbored since elementary school. Precisely the opposite happened.

Rather than causing me to further doubt and question my faith in one institution of organized religion, the Roman Catholic Church — rather than weakening my convictions about God, about a higher spiritual presence and power — The Hero With a Thousand Faces profoundly reassured me, continues to reassure me. I came to believe that it could be neither accident nor contrivance that all people — across all time, culture, and geography — would explain the world, their circumstances in it, and the journeys of their lives in exactly the same way. In that book and what it teaches, I found roots and faith.

As the centrifugal force of the earth's spinning continues to cast off depth and meaning in favor of divisiveness and superficiality, The Hero With a Thousand Faces continues to speak to me, deepening my roots and strengthening my faith. It teaches us that we are one humanity, regardless of whether we choose to heed the reality of its message.

The choice is ours to make.

* For those who don't know or who may not be ancient enough to recall, film-strip presentations comprised a strip of film, loaded into a crude projector, and advanced, frame by frame, by the person doing the presenting. The person doing the presenting was cued to advance each frame by a beep from a vinyl record, played on a nearby turntable, that did the talking so the presenter wouldn't have to. In between speeches, the record would beep, alerting the presenting person to advance the slide.

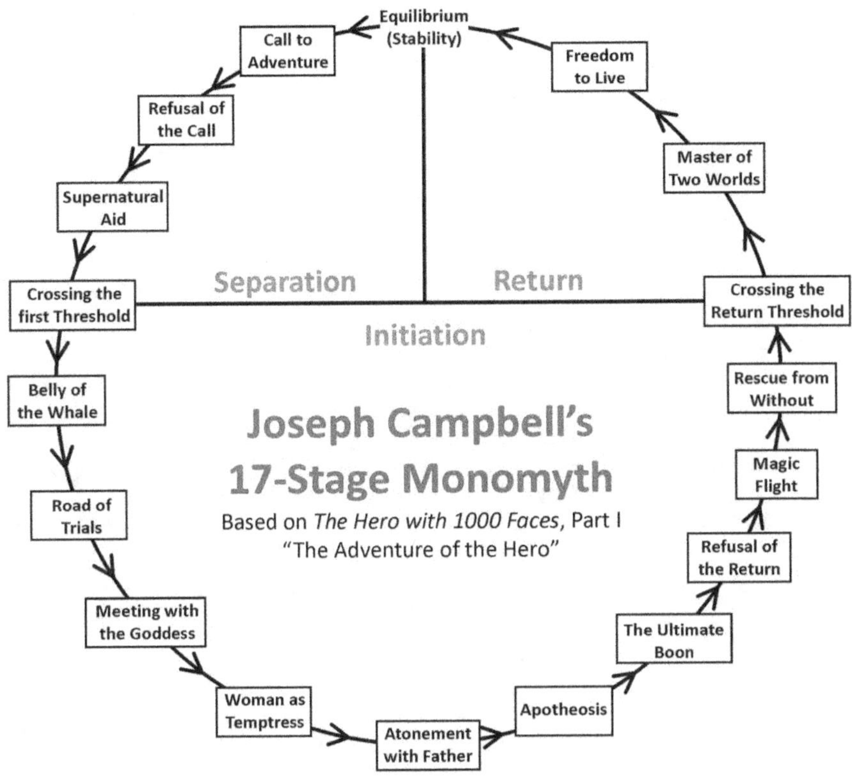

diagram courtesy of freepngandfreepdf.tk

Take the Ride

Parenthood ... It's about guiding the next generation and forgiving the last. (Peter Krause)

The ground rules: There's no blaming here. We're all making our way through the human condition. We all get the challenges and opportunities afforded by trial and error. This is the very first time down this road for each of us. But let's at least acknowledge it's all been done before. We all have the history we choose to ignore for reference. So, let's apply some common sense to — and derive some humility from — the reality that what's news to us is anything but new, including this:

Younger workers are re-inventing the conventional notion of employment, according to a survey by Deloitte ... Among millennials, 43% envision leaving their jobs within two years; only 28% seek to stay beyond five years. Employed Gen Z respondents ... express even less loyalty, with 61% saying they would leave within two years [because] business leaders' priorities don't seem to align with their own ... a majority ... agrees ... corporations 'have no ambition beyond wanting to make money' ... 62% regard the gig economy as a viable alternative ... [70%] who are members of senior management teams or on boards would consider taking on short-term contracts or freelance work as an alternative to full-time employment.

I share this because maybe, just maybe, paying attention might be preferable to being surprised. At the very least, we might be able to make some recollective progress, rather than thinking every revolution of the generational wheel is a singular and unprecedented novelty.

The fact that millennials and Gen Zers reject the work-first, company-animal psychology of their progenitors is no less predictable and no more surprising than my parents bursting into the bedroom of my teenage years screaming, "What the hell is that noise?" as I listened to Leslie West sing "Blood of the Sun" on my Zenith portable stereo with the detachable speakers. It's no less predictable and no more surprising than my bursting into the bedroom of my teenage sons screaming, "What the hell is that noise?" as they listened to Tupac rap "Hail Mary" on their boomboxes with the kidney-stone-dissolving mega-bass loosening the floor joists and rattling the china, my teeth, and my nerves. This is what we do, kids.

We resist. We rebel. We think we know better and more. We think we're the first to [fill in the blank with whatever quixotic crusade with which you or your generation were infatuated]. We think we'll re-create the world and its madness in our own images. We'll experience the same disillusionment when we find out we can't. Some of us will call the disillusionment disappointment. Some of us will call it maturity. Some of us will call it wisdom. Some of us will simply call it life.

None of us should be surprised by any of it.

Buy the ticket, take the ride. (Hunter S. Thompson)

image courtesy of pexels.com

Stranded ... and Other Blessings

Despite my Irish luck, and for the first time in my charmed life, I was recently stranded overnight in Toronto Pearson International Airport. I'd flown from Bradley International in Hartford, Connecticut, at 7:00 a.m., with a return flight scheduled at 8:55 that same evening. After a day-long meeting, I returned to the airport tired but braced by the constructive work we'd accomplished that day. I looked forward to returning home. The universe had other plans.

At the scheduled boarding time, we were invited to resume our seats in the waiting area. A short time later, we were told our plane hadn't yet arrived. Over the next three hours and 50 minutes, the story continued to morph from mechanical difficulties to the availability — then the unavailability — of another plane. At 12:45 a.m., we were told we'd be going nowhere.

The airline offered a hotel room for the night, but there were a number of catches: The next flight out, scheduled for the following morning, already was full. Ditto the flight after that, at 5:40 p.m. The next and last one of the day was scheduled to leave at 8:55 p.m. I asked the ticket agent if there were other ways out, sans finding another airline in the morning. She found a 7:00 a.m. flight to Montreal with a connecting flight to Bradley at 9:15, getting me to Connecticut at 10:30. Sold.

It was now 1:30 a.m. To take the room, I would have had to walk to the other side of the terminal, catch a shuttle, check in, and attempt to settle down enough to sleep. I'd then have to be up by or before 5:00 to be back in the terminal at 6:00 to get myself cleared for departure at 7:00. I declined the offer in favor of making the most of the next four hours or so in the airport. I went back to my seat in the waiting area, only to notice the woman who'd been seated next to me the whole time. She spoke first.

"Is your flight cancelled, too?"

I looked to my left. A woman of indeterminable age and Asian descent looked at me with soft eyes that betrayed clearly evident concern. "I'm afraid so," I responded. "Were you going to Hartford, too?"

She told me she'd missed a flight home to Wisconsin. She could have returned to her 96-year-old parents' home in Toronto. But it would've been an hour each way, and her flight was at 6:00 a.m. Retired from the medical-supply business, she'd taken a job with United Airlines because it allowed her to fly anywhere in the world for peanuts. Our conversation lasted until I walked her to her gate at 5:30 before proceeding to mine. The only pause occurred between 3:00 and 4:30, when we both dozed off.

I learned she'd lived in the United States for 43 years, after leaving Hong Kong to attend the University of Wisconsin. I learned of her family, her career, her three marriages, of jobs she'd held in Hong Kong, London, Paris, and the States. I learned of a life well-lived, and I witnessed a spirit undimmed by misfortune. I met a woman who looked younger than her years, who walked with the energetic gait and observed everything with the wondrous eyes of a child. I experienced a gentle soul, a keenly wise and curious intellect, and a generous spirit at peace with every card, good and bad, in the hand that had been dealt her.

In what had seemingly begun as just another annoying dereliction of responsibility and customer service by yet another airline, I was immeasurably enriched by my encounter with this amazing woman who'd been put on my path, at least for one enchanting night. My stranding had been a gift.

I determined to remain more vigilant for ever-present blessings.

photo courtesy of publicdomainpictures.net

It's About Time

I wonder if all of us think more about time as we grow older. I'm sure we're aware of its passing. I want to know if we share a preoccupation with what we're doing with our time. We have such a perverse relationship with it.

When we're young, there seems to be too much time. A summer day is endless if there's nothing to distract us, if we can't get access to the comic books of our best friend's older brother, if there's no mischief to instigate or risks to take.

When we get older, there's too little time. No day provides enough of it in which to eliminate our distractions, to work on the graphic novel we've been plotting since we fell in love with Stan Lee's writing, to manage the mischief — however deliberate or unwitting — of spouses and children, to find the next risk or figure out how many more we might have time to take.

How do we learn who we are if we don't take risks; if we don't challenge and re-invent ourselves; if we don't discern, discover, or develop aspects and capabilities? What beauty is there in a gem without facets?

Some of us know who we are right away. When we were in third grade, Kenny Carpenter knew he'd become an engineer at NASA. He was right. He's an engineer at NASA. Even then, I couldn't figure out how he knew. I wasn't envious, just curious.

Why didn't he do what the rest of us did – talk about becoming a doctor, or a lawyer, or President of the United States? How did he know he wouldn't become a priest, or Marilyn Manson, or Charles Manson? I'm still curious.

Was he lucky? Or did he miss the processes of discovery, re-birth, and re-invention the rest of have to struggle through, learning to live with disappointment and further re-invention when we fail, celebrating each achievement and looking forward to the next one when we succeed?

And how does Kenny manage tenses? I imagine he celebrates his past. Why not? It must be chock-full of the accomplishment that got him the gig at NASA. I imagine his present is fairly engaging, too. There must be lots of stuff to plot and calculate at NASA, right? Maybe Kenny's the guy who coaches the Expeditions to the International Space Station:

Kenny: No! Don't use the Vise Grips on that pressure gauge! Just tap the side of it with a table knife. That's how Grandma Carpenter used to loosen the lid on the cookie tin.

Astronaut: Roger that, Houston. But I thought you blew the lid off that tin with homemade C-4.

Kenny: Hey! How'd you find out about that?

It's his future I'm most curious about. Do NASA engineers learn enough to constantly re-invent themselves? I think not, since Kenny's still the NASA engineer he knew he'd become in third grade. But I don't want to sell him short. When he thinks about what he doesn't know, does it make him yearn to learn it? Does it make him consider the possibility that once he learns it, he might have to invent himself as something other than an engineer at NASA? Does the idea scare him?

It's been a long time since third grade. The idea of becoming something other than what you've always known you'll be might be a tad unnerving to a guy like Kenny. On the other hand, he'd probably think of a guy like me as just another loose screw on some cosmic space station. He probably always did.

The upshot is there are the Kenny Carpenters of the world. They have their particular, peculiar relationships with time. Then there are the rest of us. We'll never make friends with time. We'll keep working against it, like salmon against the spring run-off. We'll always be afraid there won't be enough time for the next learning, the next yearning, and where it will lead us.

We're not unhappy. We just choose to be unfinished. We work toward our next re-invention, while the clock ticks toward us from the other end. Maybe we win. Maybe the clock wins. What difference does it make? Time is all we have. And the only bad attempts are the ones not made.

We'll have plenty of time to compare notes with Kenny when the clock stops.

photo courtesy of Wikimedia Commons

Late to the Dance

My high school dating experiences were checkered, you might say.

The first formal date I recall was in my freshman year. I asked a girl in my class to go out to a movie with me. I don't remember what we saw. I don't remember how we got to the theater or how we got home. All I remember is that, sometime afterward, she told me she was embarrassed to be seen with me. I took that as her subtle way of saying she liked me and trying to boost my self-esteem.

During my sophomore year, a beautiful blonde girl in my class asked me to go to a Sadie Hawkins Dance. I don't know why she asked me. I said yes. We had an enjoyable if somewhat awkward time. I remember thinking I'd never imagined a human being smelling so good. After the dance, I never had brains enough to ask to see her again. I took that as an indication that I was an idiot.

In that same year, I dated a girl from the high school on the other side of town. I don't even remember how we met. I don't know when, how, or why we stopped seeing each other. I took that as an indication that the relationship probably didn't mean much, at least to me.

In my junior year, I dated another girl from the high school on the other side of town. I liked her very much. In fact, I liked her so much I forgot I was 17 and the world was (should have been) all opportunity. Another very beautiful girl from my class invited me to go to the Sadie Hawkins Dance that year. Because I forgot I was 17 and the world was all opportunity, I turned down her invitation. I didn't take that as confirming I was an idiot. But I should have.

For reasons I don't recall — likely insecurity and an attendant lack of caring about much of anything except altering my consciousness by various means — I didn't go to my Junior Prom or to my Senior Prom. I don't know that I was content with being an outsider. But I was an outsider. I fancied myself a latter-day Holden Caulfield — a rebellious loner, an idealistic dreamer, naïve, resentful, and positive I was misunderstood. If there'd been a category for Most Likely to Be Forgotten, I was positive I'd have been a shoo-in.

In hindsight, I suspect I was wrong about all of that. And while I recognize the futility of looking back, I also suspect I lost more opportunities than I was capable of imagining then.

As the saying goes, youth is wasted on the young.

licensed from clipartof.com

My First Boss

In 1970, when I turned 16, I went to work in a newly built McDonald's on West Main Street in Meriden, Connecticut, just a couple of doors east of Benjamin Franklin Elementary School, at which I'd been a student from Kindergarten through Fifth Grade. The manager of the store, my first real boss, was a short, pudgy Irishman named Patrick Murphy.

I distinctly remember three things about Patrick: First, he was, it seemed to me, inordinately proud of having graduated from McDonald's Hamburger University and having earned a degree in Hamburgerology. I'm sure I must have shortchanged the guy and his education, but a degree in flipping burgers, cooking French fries, and filling a machine with shake mix wasn't something that impressed me, at least at the time. In fairness, not much impressed me at the time.

Second, Patrick was every inch the affable Mick. Despite the fact that he took his degree and his job quite seriously, he took himself seriously not at all. He was unflappably affable, consistently even-tempered, and as ready to make jokes about just about anything as any member of his crew. When, on occasion, it was necessary for him to reprimand one of his employees, he was neither condescending nor abusive. He demanded nothing. Rather, he reminded us quietly and respectfully of the discipline he expected of us. That, of course (he knew), made us all the more inclined to respect him and to comply with the one set of rules to which we all adhered, including him.

Third, Patrick ate McDonald's hamburger patties raw. He said he did it to show us the purity of the product. We couldn't believe it and none of us bought his story about purity. As far as any of us knew or witnessed, he never suffered from upset stomach, nausea, diarrhea, vomiting, Campylobacter, E. coli, Salmonella, Clostridium perfringens, Yersinia, or any other bacterial hideousness he should have contracted from raw beef — to say nothing of whatever other pernicious stuff was put in those patties. I don't recall that Patrick ever even took a sick day. The dude was a 5'x5' combination of Iron Man and Superman.

SUPERFLUOUS HISTORICAL NOTE: On September 18, 1970, while I was at work at McDonald's, one of my buddies came in the front door of the store, stood just inside the door without approaching the counter, and said, "OB, Hendrix is dead." Then he walked out. It didn't matter. Neither of us would have been able to speak another word anyway.

photo courtesy of Elite Daily

My First Car

I got my first car in 1973. It was a black, 1964 Ford Galaxie with a red interior. I bought it from my father. I was 19 years old. And I was free.

I'd learned to drive in that car when I was 16. My father took me to the DMV in Middletown, Connecticut, to get my driver's license in that car. I aced the written test. My father pulled the car to the curb in front of the DMV office. My father got out. A uniformed DMV inspector got into the front passenger seat. I got into the driver's seat. It was summer. The window was open, so, I stuck my elbow out the window because I'd seen other people do it. Plus, I was cool. I started the car and drove about a foot.

The inspector said, "Stop the car."

"What's wrong?" I asked.

"I don't care what the hell you do when I'm not in the car," he said. "But when I'm in the car, keep both hands on the wheel."

Duly cautioned, I then aced the driving test.

Among my friends, that car quickly became known as The Bomber. I bought 15-inch woofers, cut 15-inch cut holes in the deck behind the back seat, and mounted the woofers underneath the deck from the trunk. I bought PA horns from Radio Shack and mounted them on the deck, alongside the holes for the woofers. Then I wired the whole rig to a huge 8-track tape player I mounted under the dash.

There were more rolling concert/parties in that car than 20 people could count using all their fingers and toes. Since all of them involved adult beverages and illegal substances, I won't recount the details of any of those parties here. But I will share another story, this one involving my father.

Dad was a Marine. Except in social situations, describing his general demeanor as stern would constitute some combination of contrived euphemism, gross understatement, and modest deceit.

One day, while driving north on the Berlin Turnpike with three of my buddies in The Bomber, another driver did something, I don't recall what, to which we all took terrific exception. My buddies decided the other driver's transgression deserved pressed hams. If you're not familiar with the pressed ham, it comprises a moon, with one's naked derriere pressed against glass. In this case, as I passed the offending driver on the left, my buddy in the front passenger seat pressed his butt against the window on his side of the car. The dude on the same side of the car in the back did the same thing in his window. The other guy in the back seat managed to get his butt pressed against the rear windshield.

As it turns out, my buddy in the front seat had powdered himself liberally that day after taking a shower. So, on the passenger side window, there was a perfect impression of his keister in white powder.

The next morning, I had to drive my father to the garage in which his car had been serviced the day before. We took The Bomber, of course. Dad got in, closed the door, and looked to his right.

"What the hell is that?" he asked … uh … sternly.

I answered his question with another question: "What does it look like?"

"It looks like somebody's ass," he said.

"Do you want to know what happened?" I asked.

"No," was all he said.

Because I'm feeling generous, I'll make the moral of the story a multiple choice contest. If you throw pressed hams in your car, the moral of the story is:

A. Don't let your buddies use powder.

B. Clean the windows afterward.

C. Don't drive your father anywhere afterward.

D. Convince your father what a blast it is to throw pressed hams in the car.

E. All of the above.

F. None of the above.

If I could get The Bomber back, I'd give the winner of the Moral Contest a ride, with the liberty of throwing an unlimited number of pressed hams, with or without powder.

I loved that car.

photo courtesy of worldcarslist.com

Frederick Exley:
1929–1992

For those who don't know his work, Frederick Exley's passing on June 17, 1992, will be as the great preponderance of the world's myriad events — unknown, unseen, unremarked. For those of us who know and love his work, his passing marked the loss of trusted eyes; of a keen and long-suffering intellect; of a voice as plaintive and hopeful as our own; of a painfully courageous honesty that even transience, alcohol, and loneliness could not extinguish; of an excruciating insight that would not have let him live or die any other way. Now that he no longer watches the world for me, I take comfort in knowing his books still hold his vision.

Aside from the occasional article and periodic piece, the body of Exley's work comprises a novelistic trilogy. Billed by the author as autobiographical fiction, *A Fan's Notes*, *Pages From A Cold Island*, and *Last Notes From Home* traverse the fuzzy line between reality and fantasy, observation and imagination, history and lies. And they draw an unsparing depiction of, as Exley characterizes it in the epigraph to *A Fan's Notes*, "that long malaise, my life".

That life was, and Exley's work reflects, an abiding struggle — eminently noble, abjectly futile, ultimately existential — to come to terms with an America so full of obscene abundance and corrupt opportunity it rendered any meaningful choosing of one's options unimaginable and any thought of personal fulfillment absurd. In Exley's America, captured in all its confounding, contradicting complexity in *Last Notes From Home*:

If nuclear arsenals had eliminated one's need to ponder a possibly nonexistent future, they had also eliminated the need to encumber oneself with literature, history, art, music, all those things we lump together under the sweeping banner of culture.

All one can do in a place so devoid of the cultural languages that define and connect us is what Exley — both man and narrative persona — did so bravely: Never quit, in the hope that coping can be an acquired skill.

But my affinity for and connection with Exley is best captured in another passage from Last Notes From Home. It describes my reasons for self-preoccupation; for bouts with depression and psychotherapy; for the often tireless need to write, to cry, to scream into keys, paper, and ink. And it explains why, for all the progress he made, Exley never mastered the skills of coping:

There is a hateful, baleful, alienating darkness in all good writers that can never be disguised by a Brooks Brothers suit, and whenever I see a good writer so got up, he always seems to me to exude the notion of soiled undergarments and fouled socks.

This sentence sums the difference between good writing and bad; that is, seasoned versus sophomoric, informed versus pretentious or superficial, visceral versus mechanical. The argument can surely be made that good writers hate nothing and no one quite so much as themselves, hence their relentless compulsion to write, to get themselves off their own chests. But good writers measure and test us, challenge our complacencies, and remind us that peace is the province of those without critical faculties — or those who choose not to use them.

With his own acute faculties, his vigilant distrust of even the most innocuous (or necessary) complacencies, and his ceaseless desire to write and be recognized for it, Exley never tested anyone as severely as he tested himself. He recognized in *A Fan's Notes*:

Though it is indeed best to keep one's devils within, one still has to learn to live with them.

For him, writing seemed to be a means of pulling those devils from his guts and hauling them out into the light in which their hideousness might diminish, in which Exley might examine them to determine if they could, in fact, be lived with.

While he struggled to the end to learn to live with those devils, he seemed to hold even that learning at bay, lest lessons learned equate to complacency in himself. Though he longed for the world to hail him as a good writer, he seemed to fear even that acclaim, contemplating later in the same novel:

How fantastically inventive life was, how terrifying really in that it sometimes does give substance to our airy dreams. And really, what good are dreams if they come true?

Finally, for all the compulsive passion in his writing, though he could no more prevent his writing than he could force it, he never admitted to its being his calling. For this, too, *A Fan's Notes* has an explanation, one that kept Exley forever in the category of fan, never pushing him over the line into the dreaded realm of the participant, never causing him to commit to anything that might later prove mundane or unworthy:

If it comes at all, Emerson has cautioned that one's call might not come for years. If it doesn't, he remarks it as only a reflection in the universe's faith in one's abstinence, nothing to move the heart to fret. And if, moreover, one is unable to do the world's work, sell its murderous missiles or cigarettes, as a poised, mute, and motionless man, one need not propagate the world's lies.

In the light, then, of his alienating darkness — got up in my Brooks Brothers suit and wondering if it disguises my airy and unfulfilled dreams any better than it hides my soiled undergarments and fouled socks, as unwilling to propagate the world's lies today as I was at 18 — I write these notes as a fan of Frederick Exley.

And as I reflect on his work, as I ponder the relationships between dreams and self-defeat, as I search vainly for direction signs in the frozen limbo between choices in which Exley also lived, as I wonder at my own calling, I think of him often ... and watch the world alone.

photo courtesy of exploringupstate.com

The Will O'Leary Rule

During the years I spent toiling for an advertising agency, the ego of the high-flying gentleman who owned the establishment fancied charter flights. In fact, to impress an adolescent nephew, Il Grande Formaggio once chartered a jet to fly us to a meeting in Cleveland, took the nephew on the flight, and had the cabbie who drove us from the airport to the meeting drop the nephew off at the Rock and Roll Hall of Fame. Le Gros Fromage had to replace his entire hat collection after that momentous trip.

Most times, though, he chartered small prop planes at a local airstrip. One such charter, booked in the dearth of commercial flights available in the immediate aftermath of 9/11, took us to Richmond to meet with a prospect. The small plane sufficed: It's less important to impress a prospect than it is to convince your teenage nephew you're The Man.

A Tangent

Two things are true of me: (1) I fall asleep readily on planes, frequently being out like a light before being airborne. (2) I disdain seat belts, on planes, in cars, anywhere. Aside from the fact that they make me uncomfortable, I once witnessed an event that solidified my anti-restraint stance:

Driving south on I-91 in Connecticut with my two then-young sons in the car, a station wagon in the left lane and a sedan in the middle lane attempted to switch lanes with each other at the same time. Recognizing their tactical error simultaneously before they collided, the drivers of the cars jerked their respective steering wheels. The driver in the sedan in the middle lane veered violently but safely into the right lane. The driver in the station wagon, the suspension of which responded as if it were manufactured of old bedsprings and marshmallows, yanked her steering wheel hard left toward the median. The car responded by barrel-rolling off the highway and onto the grassy median between the north- and south-bound lanes of traffic. As the car rolled across the median, the driver-side door was thrown open by centrifugal force, ejecting the driver upward, directly perpendicular to the ground, as the car rolled away beneath her. She landed safely and unharmed in the grass on the median as the car continued to roll, across the median and onto the other side of the highway, at which point it was struck by a northbound tractor-trailer rig and pretty much disintegrated.

Lesson learned.

Back to Our Story

At any rate, we undertook our flight to Richmond heedless of the fact that there were violent thunderstorms the length of the Eastern Seaboard. In my characteristic state of oblivion, I was comatose before the plane's three wheels ever pried themselves free from the tarmac.

At one point during the flight, the plane was rocked so violently — percussion from a thunderclap? a wind shear? generic aviatic turbulence? — my belt-less body was hurled upward (or the plane was hurled downward) causing me to wallop my noggin on the ceiling of the cabin ... and even waking me up.

I put my hands to my head, making a quick check of my scalp to ascertain whether I'd suffered a laceration. I found a decent-sized mouse on the top of my coconut, but no broken skin or blood. (If I hadn't whacked my thick, Irish skull, I might have been killed ... or worse.) I also made a quick check of my shorts to make sure I was still sanitary. Then I decided it might be prudent to panic. At the very least, it seemed as if a simmering terror might not be completely out of line.

But before panicking or surrendering to stark terror, I looked forward to the young dude in the cockpit. He was cool as a cuke.

While this might have qualified as rank rationalization, been a textbook example of wishful thinking, or been tantamount to a furtive search for the proverbial silver lining, I arrived at what seemed at the time to be two fairly sensible conclusions:

(1) The young dude in the cockpit knew a hell of a lot more about flying that plane than I did. (2) If he wasn't rattled, let alone terrified, there was no reason for me to be.

Denouement

When we were safely grounded in Richmond, I went up to the cockpit, congratulated the young dude on his aeronautical acumen, thanked him for his grace under what I took to be a completely new spin on atmospheric pressure, shook his hand, and asked him his name.

"Will O'Leary," he said matter-of-factly, without artifice or self-consciousness.

And, so, was the Will O'Leary Rule born. (The Will O'Leary rule is alternatively known as WWWD — What Would Will Do?)

Now, any time I'm on the verge of any calamity, catastrophe, or cataclysm, I look for one person who appears to be fully composed — or blissfully ignorant. I don't care. I don't attempt to judge the person's cognitive acuity. I don't look for signs of sentience. I don't check for vital signs. I just take comfort and go back to sleep.

No worries. No seat belt.

Thank you, Will.

courtesy of public-domain-photos.com

Joe Willie, Santa, and Sisyphus

Every year, in the eight weeks between Christmas and Valentine's Day, a number of things can be counted on to take place. Each is a measure of our inexplicable humanity:

First, the holiday season will vanish, leaving us to realize our spirits are none the kinder, fuller, or more generous than they were last year and to wonder what constitutes the bigger mystery: That hearts dead from distraction and routine, empty and indifferent, can be brought to joyous life, made full to beneficence by the contagious, communal majesty of a Christmas Eve service? Or that those same, full hearts can be so quickly and completely desiccated, dead as dust in the reflexive resumption of the world's hostile, unforgiving business?

Second, Martin Luther King Day will come with the renewed hope that we can understand and stop harming each other. It will pass with renewed disillusionment and the realization that we cannot. We will, again, pick up our guns, our stones, our pens, our voices, and resume the incessant vitriol that marks us human. The best intentions, the sincerest wishes, the costliest sacrifices will be lost in the Law of Large Numbers: If more people are angry and reactive than reasoning, patient, and willing to negotiate compromise, the angry and reactive will prevail.

Third, the tab will come due for all the holiday cheer we purchased, including payments deferred for gifts on which we over-spent, diets abandoned for meals we over-ate, hangovers staved by hair of the dog to keep us primed for every party of which we had to be the life. Our bank accounts dwindle while our bodies bloat. Our judgment falters as our minds fog and our livers shrivel and harden. Our gaiety becomes increasingly forced as it becomes further mortgaged.

Finally, there will be a Super Bowl. This mockery of gamesmanship will take place because our abilities to rationalize and our determination to deceive and entertain ourselves have no limits. By the time the players are lined up for kick-off, millions of us, variedly assembled in chairs, couches, family rooms, and bars all across the Land of Opportunity, will hold our breath, our wagers, and our disbelief, firm in the conviction that the hapless exercise we are about to witness might actually be a contest.

In a singular concession to our naiveté, by the same stubbornly hopeful innocence that allows us to believe in Santa Claus and the other fleeting miracles of the Christmas season just past — in the ardor-inducing magic of roses and chocolates on Valentine's Day — we'll convince ourselves the game has meaning. Like the back of Sisyphus bending under the rock, Joe Willie Namath's already stooped shoulders bow more each year for lugging the load of the dream he made manifest in his Jets' 1969 victory over Don Shula's Colts. We, too, know the painful weight of sustaining dreams. But on we push.

In weighing salary caps, binding arbitration, ticket prices, schedules, expansion teams, rules, re-plays, referees, and the myriad minutia of the game, I wonder if NFL Commissioner Roger Goodell ever thinks about the Super Bowl this way. And I wonder if perhaps, by this absurdly brutal sport made ridiculously Big Business — having ridden out one year's disappointments but looking straight into those of the next — I wonder if we don't somehow redeem ourselves by this annual rite.

Hopeful, resilient as children, we turn on The Big Game. The interminable pre-kickoff advertising space becomes, not a test of endurance, but training camp, the re-birth of our hope and our prospects, the starting point, the New Year, the time at which, with no losses on our records, we can choose to believe (or believe we can choose) whether we will win or lose. Millions of us, in a hush not heard since Christmas Eve, are compelled, as one, to hope. Wow! NFL Charities never intended anything like this.

Maybe, after tragedy upon disaster upon calamity, after another year of avoidance and denial, this high-stakes contention over a pigskin is an indication of faith. Maybe our bestowal of credence on professional football — a commercial product, and a cynical one at that — is evidence of the inherent good by which we continue to hope for the hopeless. Maybe it's some (any) measure of the possibility that our capacity for hope might endure.

And maybe, just maybe, if we allow it to, the charade we're determined to see as The Big Game might remind us why we need heroes to believe in.

Even if those heroes are gone or imagined — Joe Willie, Santa, and Sisyphus —the hope they inspire is real. On we push.

P.S. In Super Bowl III, Sisyphus took the Jets and the points.

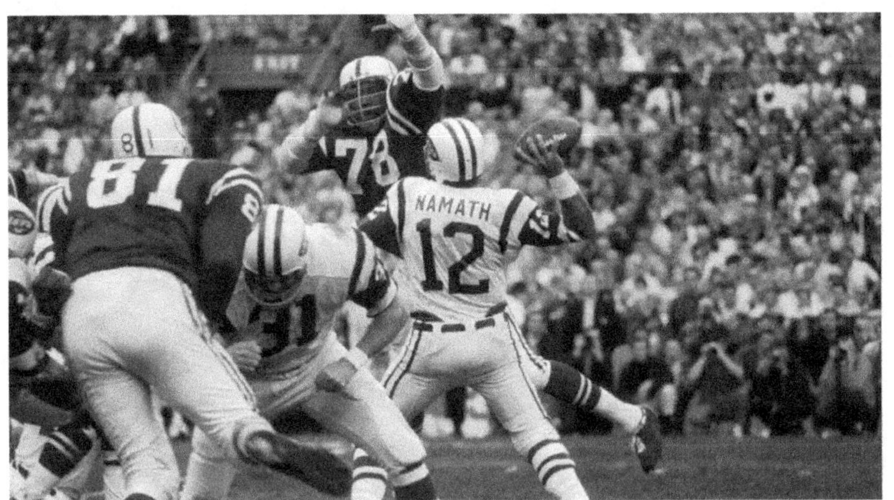

©2014 latimes.com

Eddie's Broken Tales

In October of 2017, Anne and I adopted a dog from the Connecticut Humane Society. He was a Chihuahua and French Bulldog mix. He was about a year-and-a-half old. He weighed nine pounds, soaking wet.

The first thing I need to do every morning is to sit and write something, just to find out how I am, to get a feel for how I fit in the world that day. The first thing our dog, Eddie, needs to do every morning is to walk the loop that comprises our community, just to find out how things are in his world, to see who might be up, out, and about that day.

One morning, during his morning constitutional, Eddie was walking in the mode that compels Anne and me to call him Mr. Pokey. (Anne can sometimes get Eddie to move along by speaking to him in Italian. He's particularly responsive to, "*Andiamo.*") He was taking his time, sniffing just about everything, strategically marking his turf, and checking to see if any of the soft touches were out in the neighborhood to give him treats and water, as they're wont to do.

Rather than trying to hustle Eddie along, I decided to let him do his thing, at his own pace. I pulled out my phone, checked my LinkedIn app, and found a podcast from my wonderful friend, Diane Wyzga. It was part of her weekly Wednesday series, *Stories From Women Who Walk*. The title of the story I listened to as Eddie poked along was, Story Walking the Labyrinth. This is part of what I heard:

Decades of story and communication coaching work have taught me that walking is the best way to draw a story out of ourselves or someone else. Where you walk doesn't matter. All that matters is you walk and listen out the story that wants to be heard.

Since I sensed Eddie might be experiencing a little Sniffer Fatigue, I asked him if he'd like to give his beak a break and tell me a story. He said he would. And he did.

He told me how he was abandoned in Cherokee County, North Carolina. He told me how he'd come to have his tail broken, how he'd spent weeks out in the elements, how he'd foraged for food and hidden what he could find until he could eat it in solitude and safety.

He told me about being rescued by the Cherokee County Humane Society. He told me how he'd been packed into a crate, how his crate had been packed into a truck with dozens of others, how he'd endured the long ride from North Carolina to Connecticut, and how he'd arrived at the Connecticut Humane Society location in Newington, Connecticut, road-weary but undaunted.

He told me that, due to severe malnutrition, the veterinary staff at the Connecticut Human Society had performed a dental procedure on him that cost him eight teeth. He told me about being neutered and getting the little tattoo on his belly that indicates he'd been neutered (as if his missing parts wouldn't be enough evidence). He told me about being chipped, so he'd never be lost again. He told me that, before Anne and I adopted him, he'd received the best care and the most kindness he'd ever experienced while he was in Newington.

He told me the reason he'd fought so hard to stay awake during his first night with us was that he was afraid if he let himself doze off, we'd be gone when he woke up. He told me he trembled violently when we first started taking him in the car with us because he thought we were going to ditch him again. He told me the reason he used to circle to his left around his food bowl when we fed him, all the time looking over his right shoulder, is that he was afraid he'd get beaten while he was eating. He told me the reason he loves Sammy so much is that he never thought he'd have a big brother, and he doesn't care if his brother's a cat.

He apologized for the cookies we find hidden in deep-pile bathmats, behind cushions on the sofa, and in piles of dirty laundry if we happen to put the laundry down before it goes in the washing machine. He apologized for the strip of dried beef he once left under our son Sean's pillow after Sean visited us in Connecticut. And he promised he'd always find and eat every one of the treats he hides, as long as we promised to always understand why he hides them.

When he finished his story and I picked him up, he didn't ask me why I was crying. He doesn't have time to wonder about such things. He has too many broken tales left to tell.

Thank you for reminding me to listen to him, Diane.

©Mark Nelson O'Brien

Gonzo But Not Forgotten

Hunter S. Thompson died by his own hand on February 20, 2005. I found out at about 10:00 the next morning. Despite my brute incomprehension of what I was reading, it struck me as a rather Thompsonesque moment: It was snowing — bleak, cold. I'd gone to my browser's home page to check the local weather forecast, and Thompson's death was one of the AP headlines.

My first thought was of reading Thompson's work, of all the reverent conversations I'd had with friends and colleagues about Thompson's incisive intellect and his ruthless honesty. Those memories stay with me always. The fact that we often idealized his work — that it made us wish to be possessed of the same kind of apocalyptic voice, to be the same kind of incendiary conscience — sometimes haunts me still.

Nixon was so crooked that he needed servants to help him screw his pants on every morning.

My second thought was of the price exacted from those endowed with such prophetic voices, visions, or propensities. In our conversations, my friends and I had talked about the likelihood that Thompson would have been killed had he lived in another place or time. We never extended that topic to the likelihood that it becomes impossible to live — like Jesus, Socrates, Chet Baker, Frederick Exley, and Jerzy Kosinski, or those minced by the celebrity machine like Jimi Hendrix, Heath Ledger, Michael Jackson, Amy Winehouse, Whitney Houston, et al. — when one is possessed of such voices, visions, or propensities.

Absolute truth is a very rare and dangerous commodity in the context of professional journalism.

It's not the possession that undoes the possessed. It's the things neglected, sacrificed, or disdained in deference to the possession that conspire to take them from lives so singularly unbalanced. It's easier to withdraw than it is to reach out. It's easier to scorn than it is to accept or to be accepted. It's easier to wrap oneself in work, ideology, and compulsion than it is to be vulnerable and to belong. What appears to be courage reveals itself to be a frequently fatal fear.

In a world of thieves, the only final sin is stupidity.

The possessed represent for us many things — ideals, extremes, taboos, single-mindedness we can't afford, personal asceticism we can't abide, a lack of courage and self-awareness we can't tolerate. That's why we marry, have children, form friendships, compromise, trust, and say 'yes' to the whole ride, regardless of our inability to like or control every dip and turn. Drugs, alcohol, and myriad other self-abuses are not the prices of imbalanced lives: they're the band-aids and the crutches. They're not the coping: they're the obliteration.

Hunter Thompson chose to obliterate himself. I miss his voice.

His death taught me the lesson of his life.

photo courtesy of freerepublic.com

Tell Your Story

A few years ago, Peter Guber, chairman and CEO of Mandalay Entertainment, wrote this in Harvard Business Review, "Critical details, data, and analytics are more effectively emotionalized and metabolized by the listener when they're embedded in a story." Similarly, Jonathan Gattschall wrote this in his book, *The Storytelling Animal: How Stories Make Us Human*:

The storytelling mind is a crucial evolutionary adaptation. It allows us to experience our lives as coherent, orderly, and meaningful. It is what makes life more than a blooming, buzzing confusion ... most of what is actually in fiction is deeply unpleasant [serving as a] powerful and ancient virtual reality technology that simulates the big dilemmas of human life.

What do those two statements tell us? They tell us the very stories we're like to dismiss, simply because they're ours, are powerful and ancient virtual reality technology. Imagine that.

As human beings, we're creatures that engage and compel each other by telling stories. It's what we've always done. *Beowulf* and *The Epic of Gilgamesh* (to name just two) are stories that pre-date writing. But they remain available to us because, through myth and history, they continue to teach. As the purveyors of social-media Newspeak constantly remind us, content is king. It's always been king because we've always been storytellers.

Try to imagine a headline, regardless of how compellingly it may be composed, competing with a well-told story. That headline may be more effectively persuasive to some creatures. But not us. We're human. Our history and all of our predispositions are about telling, learning from, and responding to stories. In that sense, social media — the focus on content — brings us back to the future: What's important is your story. And your story is your brand.

In the Spring 2012 edition of Wilson Quarterly, Tom Vanderbilt wrote an article entitled, "The Call of the Future", about the telephone. It's a device that could only have been invented by a race of storytellers. It transformed our ability to communicate utterly. It transformed our means of communicating not at all:

We have been fretting about the phone for years, even as it has moved closer and closer to us — once relegated to the back hallway — "between the dirty linen hamper and the gasometer," — now in our pockets. But it is difficult to say, as it seems to be morphing once more as a cultural form, whether the telephone has profoundly changed us in any way.

It's a wonderful thing to realize: We've created tools and media that have revolutionized our ability to connect with each other. We've made the world smaller and our access to it bigger. We've taken science that would once have been considered magic and made it mundane. We've smashed time and space as obstacles to communication. Yet we still communicate in the same ways we did before fire, let alone the first electronic spark: We tell stories.

So, go tell your story. You just might help yourself or someone else with the big dilemmas of human life.

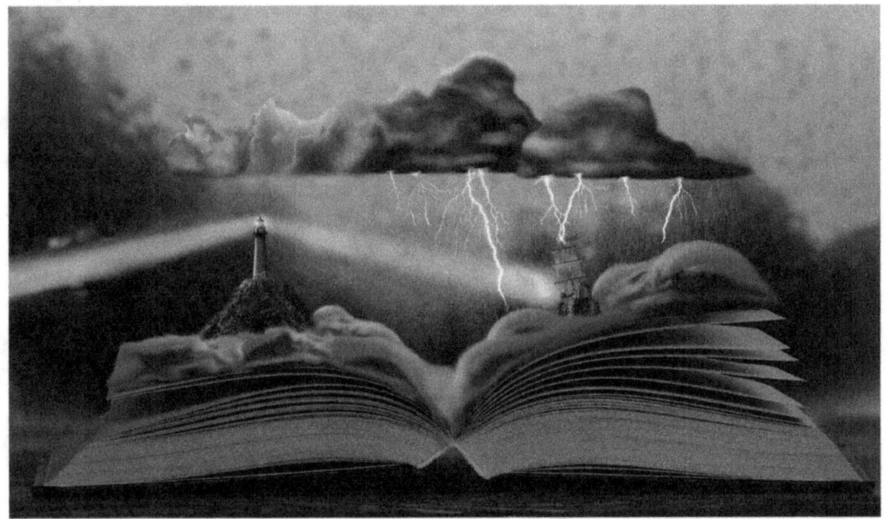

image courtesy of pixabay.com

The Big Prize

I've only won one thing in my life. It was almost as accidental as it was incidental.

I lived in Westbrook, Connecticut, from 2006 to 2015. On one of my not infrequent trips up Route 153 to Essex Wine and Spirits, I happened to see a guitar, finished like an ice-cold can of Heineken beer — complete with drops of condensation — hanging from the ceiling.

I asked the proprietor, "What's that?"

He said, "A guitar."

I took a deep breath and said, "Okay. Why is it hanging there?"

He said, "Because we're having a Heineken promotion."

"Yes," I said. "And what will happen to that guitar when the Heineken promotion is over?"

He said, "We're going to give it away."

"And how," I asked, "will you determine to whom you'll give it?"

He said, "We're having a drawing."

Recognizing the proprietor as being like many of the people with and for whom I've worked, from whom you have to pry every piece of information piecemeal, I asked: "And how might one go about entering such a drawing?"

He said, "Go up to the counter. Fill out one of those little slips of paper. And put it in the box."

I said, "Thank you," and did as I was told.

About eight or ten weeks later, I was at home. My phone rang. When I answered, the gentleman on the other end told me he was calling from Heineken North America.

I said, "I'm sorry, sir. You must have the wrong number."

He said, "You're Mark O'Brien, aren't you?"

I assured him I was.

He said, "Do you know Essex Wine and Spirits?"

I said, "Yes! Is this about that guitar?!"

He said, "Yes! You won it!"

I said, "What do I have to do to get it?"

He said, "Show up with a valid ID and take it home."

I said, "Thank you," and did as I was told for the second time in eight or ten weeks.

©Mark Nelson O'Brien

Family Traditions

WARNING: This post involves my brother, Keith (see "The Scale of Reactive Behavioral Modes"); therefore, it will, of necessity and by definition, contain bad words. Read it at risk to your finer sensibilities.

I acquired my first road bike in the summer of 2006, a Trek 5200 OCLV. At the same time, I acquired all the necessary accouterments, including shoes with cleats on them for my clipless pedals, a helmet, spandex shorts with chamois in the seats, and any number of gaudy cycling jerseys.

I was living in Middletown, Connecticut, at the time. Keith lived in Meriden, an adjoining town, which also happens to be our hometown. Early one evening, I took advantage of the late sunset to ride to Keith's house to tell him how much I'd enjoyed his son's wedding the weekend before. When I pulled up in front of Keith's house, he happened to be out in the front yard doing some trimming.

Looking up from his labors, he said: "Who the fuck are you supposed to be, Lance Armstrong?"

By the winter of 2014, Keith was living in New Haven with his girlfriend, Hanna. One day, for reasons I can't recall and that are immaterial now, Keith and Hanna invited me to visit them for dinner. It was one of those typical New England winter days in which the sky spits a stinging combination of rain, sleet, and snow. To protect my head and to keep my trifocals dry, I wore a wide-brimmed fedora. I got out of my car, ascended the front steps, and rang Keith's doorbell.

When he came to the door, he said: "Who the fuck are you supposed to be, Indiana Jones?"

On Thanksgiving Day of 2020, Anne and I flouted COVID conventions and invited Keith and Hanna to celebrate with us. Since, left to his own devices, Keith can tend to be rather solitary, Anne and I were grateful he'd accepted our invitation. He and Hanna arrived, as previously arranged, promptly at 1:00 p.m. and rang the bell. I went to the door, sporting the beard I'd grown since the last time Keith and I had seen each other.

He said, "Who the fuck are you supposed to be, Grizzly Adams?"

We all have our quirks. Our quirks inform our traditions. And one of Keith's traditions is to be verbally abusive, without regard to race, creed, color, religion, sexual orientation, gender identification, or familial relation. That's why I love the guy so much. And it's why I laugh all the harder every time he's true to his traditions and to himself.

Sticks and stones may break my bones, but Keith's words reassure me everything's right with the world.

©Mark Nelson O'Brien

I Have a Dream

"I'd walk a mile over hot coals to [fill in the blank]." "I'd crawl a mile over broken glass to [fill in the blank]."

How many times have you heard statements like that? Certainly, there's a proliferation of love-related songs and sentiments that echo such lofty, self-challenging notions. But when push comes to shove, how many of us are ready to bear the real and frightening burdens of such tests?

Aye, there's the rub.

There are two schools of thought on the topic. The first comes courtesy of a gentleman with whom I used to work. He loved to say, "If you don't have dreams, all you have is nightmares." He was right, course. Even unfulfilled dreams sustain us in difficult times. And seemingly unreachable dreams afford us positive distractions from unpleasant realities.

The second school of thought is a little less hopeful; although, I suspect most of us have experienced enough disappointment to wonder at the power of fulfilled dreams to satisfy. At the end of *The Great Gatsby*, F. Scott Fitzgerald wrote:

I thought of Gatsby's wonder when he first picked out the green light at the end of Daisy's dock. He had come a long way to this blue lawn and his dream must have seemed so close that he could hardly fail to grasp it. He did not know that it was already behind him, somewhere back in that vast obscurity beyond the city, where the dark fields of the re- public rolled on under the night.

The contemplation, then, becomes this: What do you want? How badly do you want it? What are you willing to give or pay or sacrifice to get it?

More simply: What are you willing to do to realize your dream(s)?

image courtesy of pixabay.com

Thanksgiving

The celebration of our American Thanksgiving Day got me thinking about where we are, where we've been, and what we've lost.

Before they became allergic to the Western Europeans who founded the United States, the politically incorrect pages of our history books taught us the first Thanksgiving feast was held in the autumn of 1621 by the Pilgrims (the marauding bad guys) and the Wampanoag tribe (the aboriginal good guys) to celebrate the Plymouth Plantation's first successful harvest.

But we don't celebrate our history anymore. We don't celebrate the things that unite us and for which we should be thankful. We celebrate and flaunt our differences, be they ethnic, religious, political, or personal. Listening and sharing? No, thanks. We'll take doggedness and dogma. We've lost much.

According to the New World Encyclopedia:

A tribe is viewed, historically or developmentally, as a social group existing before the development of — or outside of — states. Many anthropologists used the term tribal society to refer to societies organized largely on the basis of kinship.

Theoretical debates notwithstanding, one word in that definition denotes the one thing we've lost and sorely lack: kinship.

To be of the American tribal kin is a choice. To recite its Pledge of Allegiance is a choice. To revere its flag is a choice. To doff one's cap, to stand at attention, and to hold one's hand over one's heart during its National Anthem is a choice. To be united in all of those activities is a choice. To be thankful for that unity is a choice. But they don't appear to be the choices we're making.

Baby picks off your plate. Yours looks better.
And she throws hers on the floor.
Here, in the home of the brave
And the land of the free,
The first word baby learns is more.
(Don Henley, "Gimme What You Got", from End of the Innocence)

We might not be sure what we want. But we know we want more of it. We want it now. And we're not giving thanks for anything — or to anyone — until we get it. So, what to do?

An old axiom says, "Sincerity is everything. Once you learn to fake that, you got it made." Here's a less cynical alternative: Joy is everything. Once you learn to fake that, you got it made. It's less cynical because faking sincerity can't possibly make us sincere. But faking joy just might make us thankful, even if it only creates opportunities to share. Have you ever shared anything without being thankful? There's even gratitude in shared pain. Isn't that why misery loves company?

No more energy is expended in faking joy than in holding fast to close-minded conviction. So, what's to lose? Let's try faking joy, even if we only do it for one day. It won't cost us anything we're not already expending. It may even cost substantially less.

As we invent more modes of communication, we become less communal. As we create more electronic connections, we abandon our human ones. As we separate, we fail to share. As we worship the physical, the spirit withers. As we defy rites of passage, we fight our inevitable passing. As we create more fears, we forsake joy. As we forsake joy, we eradicate thankfulness.

Give thanks. I'll try if you will. It's the least we can do as members of our tribe.

image courtesy of freepik.com

Take the First Step

When I speak to students during readings of my books, *Martin the Marlin*, *The One and Only Ben*, and *Martin the Marlin: Friends Help Friends* — in groups that often number in the hundreds, from Kindergarten through 8th grade — I get questions so direct they can only come from children. One of the questions I get most frequently is this: "How do I become a writer?" My stock answer is that you have to do two things:

Write.

Don't quit.

At one such engagement, a young man in 5th grade asked the question. When I said, "Write," he started to smile. When I said, "And don't quit," his smile widened, his eyes lit up, and he positively beamed. He replied, "I'll never quit!" I looked at his face. Then I glanced at the face of his teacher. Then I looked back to the boy. I said to his teacher, "Look at that young man's face. The only thing he's going to do is succeed. And he knows it." His teacher then smiled and replied, "Yes, he does."

Along our respective ways, how do we lose that kind of simple certainty? I don't think it's stolen from us. I think we surrender it.

What could be worth a concession that profound? What could be so powerful as to compel us to abdicate our creative confidence? Is it fear? Are we afraid to be judged? Are we reluctant to create because we think our efforts will fall short, even — perhaps especially — in our own estimations? If we do acquire a fear of failure, it's more dangerous than it is sad.

It's dangerous because if we're not creating, we're conforming. Our choices are the beaten path or the road not taken. Granted, not everyone is temperamentally inclined to create randomly, to start businesses, or to defy the status quo. But what convinces us to forego our self-reliance in deference to the notion that we have to go along to get along?

Spending time with children makes you realize how easily adults accept defeat.

Many children also ask, "What should I do first?" Many adults ask the same question. Answer? It doesn't matter. Paying undue attention to the first step makes it the source of paralyzing anxiety if we assume it has to be perfect. It doesn't. The first step is, indeed, the most important — but only because, without it, there can't be a second or a third.

Do you need to plan the trip? Yes. Do you need to know the destination? No. Plan the trip. Take the first step. Stop. Breathe. Look around. Think. If things look exactly as you imagined them, take the second step. If they don't, allow for the change, amend the plan, then take the second step. For subsequent steps: lather, rinse, repeat.

I had no idea writing and publishing books for children would open doors to their schools. It wasn't in the plan. But I took enough steps to see the opportunity. So, I amended my plan and followed the opportunity. That's really all it takes.

If you don't believe that, let me know. I'll invite you to join me at the next school I visit.

You'll see the truth in every young face in the room.

©Mark Nelson O'Brien

Blessed With Challenges

In 2004, the priest who presided over the high-school graduation of my son, Quinn, said this, acknowledging the myriad difficulties of the age in which the accidents of our births find us in existence: "We are blessed with challenges."

My first reaction was something along the lines of, "Whoa! Sounds like the padre's gone off his meds."

Even after giving what he'd said considerable thought, it took me a while to catch his drift. But I finally made sense of it by posing a question to myself: Would you rather be challenged or bored? After that, everything fell into place ... and stayed there.

I understood why I don't sleep well — or believe I don't. I understood why I need to be occupied, almost all the time, with something, anything, preferably something creative. I understood why I find it absurd, bordering on insulting, when someone asks me, "Why don't you relax?" And I came to peace with the reality that I'm only at peace when I'm constructively engaged.

Then another shard of light glinted from the haystack of contemporary communication, a haystack that obscures with its sheer, incalculable volume. I was fortunate enough to spot it nevertheless — an article in Financial Times — "The Joy of Stress" — with the temerity to observe human nature, to tell the truth about it, and to celebrate it without trying to change it.

The article said this, in part:

There is a particular vitality in anxiety, a sort of nervy power that one can't say is fun, exactly, but is nonetheless slightly addictive. It can be productive, in a crashing way. It gives us a feeling of motion, of momentum, of wheels turning. One gets used to it, maybe seeks it out. One inhabits it, sets up camp.

Nervy power. Motion. Momentum. Wheels turning. There it is, in all its creative glory.

The physiological signs of that vital anxiety — of the creative rush — are unmistakable. I feel butterflies in my stomach, the telltale tingle that makes it impossible to do or to concentrate on anything else. My heart rate accelerates, perhaps because of adrenaline, palpable and energizing. Then comes the crystal-clear realization that anything and everything I was otherwise supposed to be doing should be dropped in deference to the tireless pursuit of the Muse, regardless of day or time.

In the song, "It's All Right, Ma (I'm Only Bleeding)", Bob Dylan observed, "He not busy being born is busy dying." One state precludes the other: being born (creating) or dying (stagnating). No judgment. Only observation. For those not called to create, there may be joy in stagnation, in the lack of vital anxiety. But for the rest of us, in the absence of that anxiety, there's only the sense that we're missing something.

I don't know if folks like me are right. I don't know if we've found the secret to life well-lived or if we'd claim uninterruptedly blissful contentment. But I do know we're fulfilled, even if we are a little stressed sometimes.

We wouldn't have it any other way.

image courtesy of pixabay.com

The Will O'Leary Rule: Part Two

A couple of chapters ago, I published Part One of this series. There won't be another one.

On Thursday, September 2, 2021, twenty years on from the story I related in that earlier story, almost to the day, Will O'Leary was killed in a crash, doing what he loved most.

I didn't know Will beyond the time I spent flying with him, even though those occasions were fairly numerous. He did, however, inform one of the philosophical convictions I've held for the last two decades: Don't worry about anything until it's really time to be worried about it.

Will had cause to be worried this time. But he didn't have much time to worry about it. The good news is he wasn't in the air long. The bad news is he wasn't in the air long. The private jet he was flying crashed into a commercial building in

Farmington, Connecticut, less than a mile from Robertson Airport in Plainville, Connecticut, from which he'd taken off.

When I was young enough to have been a Cub Scout, I was swimming in a lake at a Boy Scout camp. My younger brother got in trouble in the water. I swam toward him, dove beneath him, and pushed him up toward the pier that extended out into the lake, floating on some kind of Styrofoam cushions. As he went up, I went down. I found myself under the pier. Rather than panicked, I felt absolute serenity. I didn't think about dying at all; although, I was pretty sure the jig was up.

I heard a vague splash above me. In a moment, a lifeguard grabbed me by the arm, pulled me out from under the pier, and swam with me back up to the surface. I was grateful to have been saved. But otherwise, I didn't feel as if I'd had a close shave. What I'd experienced didn't feel anything like near-death. It just was.

I can only hope Will experienced that same serenity when he realized the odds he'd been compiling against himself when all his hours of flying time had finally reached End Game. He had to have known there was no lifeguard. He undoubtedly thought of the other people on the plane. And he likely shook his co-pilot's hand before impact. Knowing Will from having flown with him, he probably thought he could land the plane safely — if only someone would move that manufacturing plant out of the way.

Time is a very arbitrary beast. You'll never tame it. So, make the most of it.

That's my new Will O'Leary Rule.

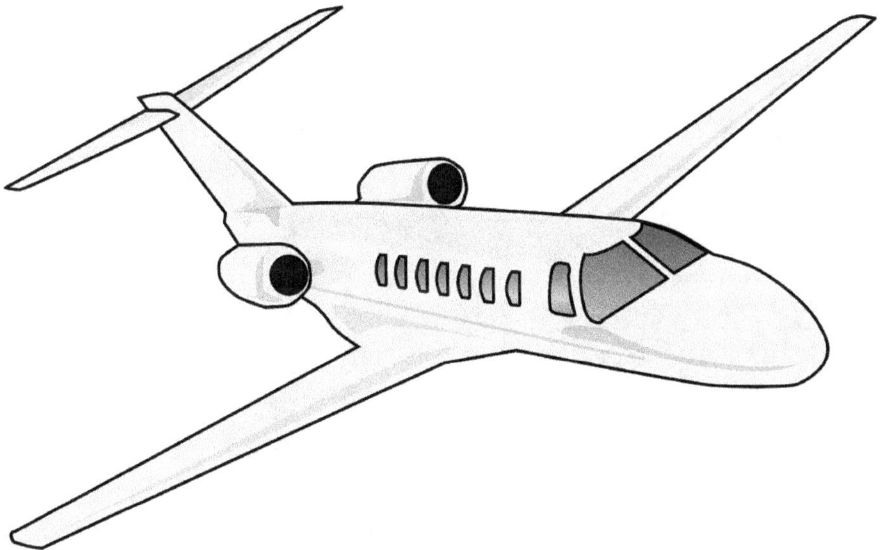

image courtesy of public-domain-photos.com

Dreams Die Hard

When I was in high school, my father had a cabinet made for me at a local trade school. It was made to accommodate the old Zenith portable stereo record player that sat on top of it. And the inside had vertical dividers to keep my collection of LPs arranged in whatever order happened to move me at any given moment. I recently came across an album in that cabinet, which is now squirreled away in my basement, that yanked me back to memories of a man who passed away in 2007 but whose personal and musical influences on me abide. In all likelihood, you've heard of neither him nor his music.

His name was Bill Chinnock. He was a product of the music scene of Asbury Park, New Jersey. (He was Bruce Springsteen before Bruce Springsteen was Bruce Springsteen. And Danny Federici, Vinny "Mad Dog" Lopez, Garry Tallent, David Sancious, and others were part of Bill's band before joining Springsteen's E Street Band. Bill's life and career later took him to New York City,

Nashville, and Portland, Maine). Bill took his own life after a long, excruciating siege of Lyme Disease and ten days after losing his mother. He was 59 years old.

I met Bill in 1977, at the Silver Bullet in Moodus, Connecticut, a club in which my band played every Thursday night. He played the Bullet several Friday and Saturday nights before moving up to more prominent Connecticut venues like New Haven's Toad's Place. In fact, I was with Bill at the Silver Bullet on his 30th birthday — November 12, 1977. We always had wonderful conversations about the business and about Bill's growth as a performer and a musician. During one of our visits, I mentioned how much his guitar playing had improved. He said he'd honed his songwriting to a point at which he was happy with it. So, he'd turned his attention to his guitar chops.

Bill met legendary producer and talent scout, John Hammond, in 1974. Hammond suggested he work on his songwriting. So, Bill left the Jersey shore and moved to Maine, refining his craft while continuing to perform and record. In 1978, he was signed by Atlantic Records, recording and releasing the album, Badlands. (Ironically, Bill's album was released just ahead of Bruce Springsteen's album, *Darkness on the Edge of Town*, which otherwise would have been called *Badlands*.)

Bill then began recording a second album for Atlantic, *Dime Store Heroes*. As the story goes, he was unhappy with the producers in the studio. So, he went and talked to the executive who was the head of the label. Bill convinced the exec to pay for building him a studio in Maine, in which Bill would finish the album and produce it himself. The exec did. And Bill did. When Bill brought the tapes to Atlantic, the exec told him Atlantic would distribute the album, but Bill should put it out on his own label, North Country Records. Then they released him from his contract, succumbing, no doubt, to the entertainment industry's unwillingness to promote anyone and anything it can't tidily and comfortably pigeonhole. (See "Danny Gatton: By the Darkness of Talent.")

It's always been hard for me to imagine that Atlantic wouldn't have wanted Dime Store Heroes in its catalog. If the label hadn't considered anything else, it should have been proud to have a song like "Baptized on 47th Street" in its holdings. After a stark intro comprising just piano and saxophone, Bill sings this poetry:

There's a baby crying
Twilight in a four-dollar room
In a garden of wallpaper flowers and roses and lilac perfume.

Later in the same song, he sings the line, "There's the wrong kind of laughter on 47th Street."

"Queen of the Lower East Side" is also worth the price of admission. In it, Bill sings:

And in the hobo jungles, I learned the truth in the eyes of the old men.
They cried, "America, you never intended me to win.

Then, in that amazing voice, he wails all the angst and frustration of the American Dream unrealized.

In the '80s, Bill moved to Nashville, still searching for the recognition that eluded him. He recorded two albums there: 1985's independent release, *Rock & Roll Cowboy*, and the 1987 CBS Records release, *Learning to Survive in The Modern Age*, which featured the single, "Somewhere in the Night." Bill won an Emmy for "Somewhere in the Night" when it was used in a daytime soap opera. He later recorded a chart-topping duet with Roberta Flack, "Hold on to Love", which was used as the theme for another soap, *The Guiding Light*.

In his live performances, Bill Chinnock owned the stage, stalking it with passion and fury, prowling it with the grace and authority of a cat, fully in command of his band, every member of which was attentive to his every move and cue. And he owned every member of every audience with his easy charm and his charismatic energy. When he played the Silver Bullet, I'd be there Friday and Saturday nights. When he played Toad's Place, I was in the front row. The wonder of his presence never diminished.

Aside from the fact that I've seen very few people commanded a stage or an audience the way Bill did (B.B. King is the only one who comes to mind), his was (in my humble estimation) THE definitive reading of the Hoagy Carmichael classic "Georgia On My Mind" (with apologies to Brother Ray). And anyone who never heard "Something for Everybody" in live performance (with the inimitable Sam Hall on tenor sax) missed a thing of beauty and wonder.

I still have the Atlantic Records release of *Badlands* on vinyl. In 2019, Bill's original recording of *Badlands* on North Country Records was released on CD. I have that, too. I also have *Dime Store Heroes* and *Out on the Borderline* (a 1992 release) on CD. And you can find Bill in the Music Museum of New England and in numerous videos on YouTube. We can only hope the Music Gods may someday draw the attention to Bill's music it's always deserved.

Bill's spirit and his music will never leave us. But I'll leave the last words in this post to Bill, from "Queen of the Lower East Side":

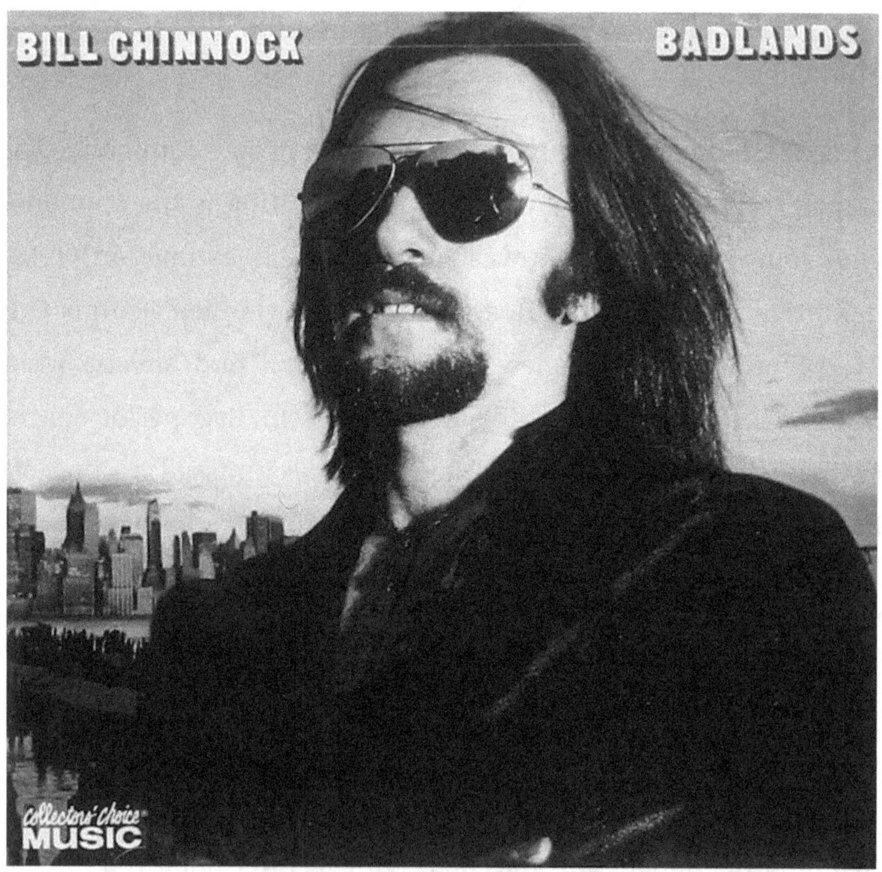

image courtesy of amazon.com

A Christmas Blessing

In the song, "Turn, Turn, Turn", made famous by the Byrds, though adapted from Ecclesiastes 3:1 by George Aber and Pete Seeger, we learn this: "To everything, there is a season and a time to every purpose under Heaven." So it is, then, that — even for me — there is a purpose for setting aside petty sarcasm for the sincerity and reverence due the season.

It's Christmas Eve. No other evening of the year is so full of wonder, of promise, of peace, hope, and humanity. If you don't know it, you can hear it. If you can't hear it, you can feel it. If you can't feel it — and presuming your lack of feeling isn't attributable to matters of religious affiliation or lack thereof — I hope this story helps.

As a recovering Catholic, troubled by the rote proscriptions and prescriptions of the faith, I'm compelled to find the relevance of the historical figure of Jesus; of his significance, even as a non-deified being; as an exemplar, rather than a judge. What's his instructive import as a mortal? Why has he attracted followers the world over for more than 2,000 years?

The simple answer is that, as a human being, Jesus suggests by his own example the extent to which we're capable of self-sacrifice. Will we be called to lay down our lives for others? Likely not. Would we be capable of doing so? That's the important question and, perhaps, the reason this time of year is called the Season of Giving.

Christian, Jew, Muslim, Hindu — we all know right from wrong. And regardless of our skin color, we're innately capable of giving.

If you're not sure of that, get the film version of Charles Dickens' A Christmas Carol starring George C. Scott as Ebenezer Scrooge. Watch it as many times as it takes. If you cry during Marley's visit to Scrooge, you'll be fine. If not, don't give up. But if you're not crying at Scrooge's visit to the graveyard with the Ghost of Christmas Future, hit Replay and start to worry. If that performance doesn't reach you, you're going to require more work.

Whatever you do, please read the speech that follows from Dickens' original text, delivered to Scrooge by his nephew on Christmas Eve. It'll remind you of your own heart and its proper place. It'll remind you of the price of hubris and the importance of humility.

It'll remind you why Christmas Eve is so full of wonder, of promise, of peace, hope, and humanity. Most important, it'll remind you of your own blessings, regardless of whether you acknowledge them, let alone be grateful:

I am sure I have always thought of Christmas time, when it has come round — apart from the veneration due to its sacred name and origin, if anything belonging to it can be apart from that — as a good time: a kind, forgiving, charitable, pleasant time: the only time I know of, in the long calendar of the year, when men and women seem by one consent to open their shut-up hearts freely, and to think of people below them as if they really were fellow-passengers to the grave, and not another race of creatures bound on other journeys. And therefore, uncle, though it has never put a scrap of gold or silver in my pocket, I believe that it has done me good, and will do me good; and I say, 'God bless it!'

I sincerely wish you the blessings of the Season, by whatever means you find them.

image courtesy of pixabay.com

Trust Yourself

If you read enough, and long enough, you're bound to come across something worth your time — the proverbial diamond in the rough; the product of a keen intellect; a thoughtful treatise, rationally conceived, soundly argued, and engagingly persuasive. The finding is as joyful as the reading.

On the website of The New Yorker, I happened on a blog post called, "The Pointlessness of Unplugging". It's written by Casey N. Cep, a wonderfully winsome writer whose wisdom beggars belief, coming from one so seemingly young. In the process of a thoughtful but thorough debunking of the fallacious notion of disconnecting from the world, Ms. Cep posits a point so salient, so intellectually engaging, so incisively and innocuously truthful, it rings in the mind:

The unplugging movement is the latest incarnation of an ageless effort to escape the everyday, to retreat from the hustle and bustle of life in search of its still core. Like Thoreau ignoring the locomotive that passed by his cabin at Walden Pond or the Anabaptists rejecting electricity, members of the unplugging movement scorn technology in the hope of finding the authenticity and the community that they think it obscures.

Magnificent. Cutting to the heart of philosophy — "Why are we here?" — and cutting through the kultursmog of faux primitivism that purports to celebrate our organic roots, even as it ignores or disdains our spiritual, mythological lineage celebrated in *The Hero With a Thousand* Faces by Joseph Campbell — Ms. Cep gives us two cogent sentences that trump the trampling trivializations of popular culture.

Ms. Cep's comment puts her in august company. Example: In his essay, "Summer in Algiers", published in 1938, Albert Camus, at the time also in his youth at age 25, wrote this:

If there is a sin against life, it consists perhaps not so much in despairing of life as in hoping for another life and in eluding the implacable grandeur of this life.

While one must hold to one's dreams, Cep and Camus point out the futility of wishful thinking. They connote the cost of eschewing reality for the unreal, which is an act of denial (as opposed to the fantastical, which is an act of imagination). It's easier to deny than to accept. It's easier to escape than to endure. It's easier to refuse than to cope. It's why we are where we are.

Our denial of reality has cost us our cultural reverence for the healing power of pain. We've forgotten that healthy growth — economic, personal, and political — productive change; deliberate, constructive restraint; and all other worthwhile things require pain, at least in this life. There's no free lunch. There are no free rides. There are only choices. Amen.

Given bleak prognoses in a world of groupthink, denial, hypocrisy, and intellectual laziness, what's to be done? Read. Read and think. Read, think, and settle for nothing. Read, think, settle not at all, and trust your own thought, as Ralph Waldo Emerson wrote in his essay, "Self-Reliance". Most important, write. Even if, perhaps especially if, you don't fancy yourself a writer, write. Your thoughts may surprise you.

If you commit yourself to those things, you too might find yourself in distinguished company. Albert Einstein wrote this in a letter to the College of the City of New York, defending the appointment of Bertrand Russell to a teaching position there:

Great spirits have always found violent opposition from mediocrities. The latter cannot understand it when a man does not thoughtlessly submit to hereditary prejudices, but honestly and courageously uses his intelligence and fulfills the duty to express the results of his thought in clear form.

In that passage, you'll find common threads, dispositional connections between thinkers of different types, linked by intellect, philosophy, honesty, and courage: Casey N. Cep, Albert Camus, Albert Einstein: By virtue of their writing, all of us are able to derive our own lessons.

Trust yourself to do so. Isn't that the point?

image courtesy of
americanpoems.com

Do It Well

When my three siblings and I were children, Mom and Dad took us to dinner at the historic Griswold Inn in Essex, Connecticut. The place was bustling, as always. Young members of the wait staff hustled from table to table, tending to their patrons.

After a few minutes, an older gentleman, dressed in wait garb, approached our table, introduced himself, asked us how we were, and inquired if any of us would like drinks of any kind before ordering our meal. Mom and Dad ordered cocktails. My siblings and I ordered soft drinks. The gentleman excused himself to submit our orders.

As the gentleman left our table with a relatively slow but deliberate gait, my Dad smiled. Knowing he wouldn't have made fun of the waiter, I asked why. Dad said admiringly, "The gentleman who just took our drink orders has forgotten more about waiting on tables than any of the younger people in here will ever know." And, so, was born my respect for a job — any job — done well.

Soon after my Dad passed away, I saw a post on LinkedIn headlined, "What the Shoeshine Guy can Teach Us About Doing a Job Well." There it was:

"Have you ever seen a Shoeshine Guy who wasn't smiling ... who didn't take extreme care in his craft and pride in his product? I'm always amazed at the meticulousness, the attention paid, and the time spent on each pair ... there's something in the process that provides satisfaction."

Of course, Dad taught us to polish our shoes. He was a Marine. He taught us you don't apply shoe polish with a brush. That's why God invented fingers. He taught us you don't worry about blackened fingers. That's why God invented soap. He taught us you don't stop brushing, by hand, until you can see your reflection in the leather. That's why God invented horsehair.

Most important, he taught us wearing those well-polished shoes — doing any job as well as we did that one — was as much a sign of regard for ourselves as it was for the people who'd know we'd done that job, any job. That's why God invented respect.

Needless to say, we resented him for it, for imposing that discipline on us. Fortunately, he lived long enough to see us become men, to understand we'd learned what he taught us, to know we revered it and understood its indelible value.

Having a father like mine made me driven, idealistic, and perfectionistic. It's been said of me more than once: "O'Brien is not a team player." I know I can speak for my siblings: They'd take that judgement as a compliment, as do I.

If the team has lost its focus, its purpose, its unity, and its direction — and if the job at hand will suffer as a result — we couldn't be less interested in the team. We'll put the job before the team every time. We won't look back. We'll regret nothing.

We compromise. But we mind the clock. There's only so much time. If you don't aspire to do the job you have at any moment to the best of your ability in every moment, you're cheating something or someone. That is NOT why God invented respect.

Every moment is a gift. Do what you do fully, in every moment. And do it well. Nothing, no one, and no job lasts forever.

Rest in peace, Dad. Thank you. Whatever I do next, I'll do it well.

©Mark Nelson O'Brien

A Thought

Thinking is the hardest work there is, which is probably the reason why so few engage in it. (Henry Ford)

A friend froze me in my tracks the other day. In the midst of a conversation we were having, he said: "I have a thought."

I couldn't believe it. I wouldn't have been surprised or found it in any way remarkable if he'd said, "I have an idea," or "How about this?" or "Check this out." But he didn't. He had a thought. And he told me so. Think about the significance of that:

I don't think we think about thinking anymore. We're too busy to think. We plan. We project. We forecast. We anticipate. We react. We plot. We scheme. We hope. We worry. We talk. Think?

We don't have the time ... or so we think. We say things like, "There aren't enough hours in the day," convinced that every one of all of our days is full. Are we sure? Is that even possible? How do we define a full day?

If you laugh, you think, and you cry, that's a full day. That's a heck of a day. (Jim Valvano)

We have more people than we need writing, talking, lecturing to and about us to be happy, to balance work and life, to work hard and play hard, to disconnect, to shut down, to blah, blah, blah, blah. We get all that.

But when's the last time anyone suggested you stop and think? That's all, just stop — then think. If we did, and if we accepted our own thinking, I wonder what kind of thoughts we'd have.

In every work of genius we recognize our own rejected thoughts: they come back to us with a certain alienated majesty. (Ralph Waldo Emerson)

What do you think we think about thinking that causes us to avoid it so? Maybe we're so conditioned to thinking we're too busy to think that stopping to think makes us uncomfortable. Maybe in the midst of lives chaotic and cacophonous, the quiet absence of commotion makes us anxious. Maybe we've become so driven by circumstances and so desperate for distraction that solitude disquiets us.

I don't know. But I think we should try it.

I want to know if you can be alone with yourself and if you truly like the company you keep in the empty moments. (Oriah Mountain Dreamer)

image courtesy of freepik.com

The Business Lessons of Literature

For man, unlike any other thing organic or inorganic in the universe, grows beyond his work, walks up the stairs of his concepts, emerges ahead of his accomplishments. (John Steinbeck, The Grapes of Wrath)

Like so many other inexplicable occurrences in my life, I somehow managed to get through an education in English Literature without reading *The Grapes of Wrath*. Is that more or less inexplicable than the fact that I also got through that same education without reading *The Count of Monte Cristo*, which is now my favorite novel? You decide.

Passages like the one above remind me, yet again, why some works endure in our literary canon, while others are relegated to remainder bins and the shelves of airport book stores. They teach us. Unfailingly, if we're willing to learn, they teach us. Even as they remind us about courage, strength, self-faith, perseverance, and transcendence — what they teach is entirely up to us.

To create today is to create dangerously. Any publication is an act, and that act exposes one to the passions of an age that forgives nothing. (Albert Camus, Resistance, Rebellion, and Death)

The business idea, like the literary idea, is an expression, a creative one. It must be. No one creates a business to be ordinary. No one creates a business to be lost in the herd. Every business is an extension of personality, of intent, of will, of hope. Businesses can't be sustained by ego. But their creation is the product of ego, as well as of intellect, imagination, and emotion. And ego remains an aspect of differentiation. The sum of any business's differentiators is its brand.

We do live in an age that forgives nothing — in a business and political climate that disdains individualism. We deny the reality of winners and losers. We think fairness, equality, and social justice are legislative products. They are not. We believe they can and should be mandated. They cannot. The history of our species teaches us that. But Utopian dreams die hard. Centralize, homogenize, patronize, organize — huddle the masses, redistribute the wealth, lower the denominators, and all will be right with the world. Such are the circumstances under which the act of creation becomes one of danger. And so it goes, until ...

If now and then we encounter pages that explode, pages that wound and sear, that wring groans and tears and curses, know that they come from a man with his back up, a man whose only defenses left are his words and his words are always stronger than the lying, crushing weight of the world, stronger than all the racks and wheels which the cowardly invent to crush out the miracle of personality. (Henry Miller, Tropic of Cancer)

There it is — the miracle of personality — the single and singularly profound miracle that gives us literature and businesses.

In the light of that miracle, the only meaningful questions are these: How do I express this? How do I create that? Why must I? The only answer is this: personality. You're driven to create or you're not. Either way is an accident of personality.

Everyone needs to make a living. Most of us would rather be financially comfortable than not. But make no mistake: No one who creates a work of literature or founds a successful business to fulfill a dream does it for the money.

People who create literature do it to share — ideas, observations, truths. People who create businesses do it to share — ideas, opportunities, rewards. Like literature, good businesses create environments for learning, for interpreting, for growing, for giving people — who may not have the need to create — a chance to discover the miracles of their own personalities.

Great ideas come into the world as quietly as doves. Perhaps then, if we listen attentively, we shall hear, among the uproar of empires and nations, the faint fluttering of wings, the gentle stirrings of life and hope. Some will say this hope lies in a nation; others in a man. I believe rather that it is awakened, revived, nourished by millions of solitary individuals whose deeds and works every day negate frontiers and the crudest implications of history. Each and every one, on the foundations of their own suffering and joy builds for all. (Albert Camus)

image courtesy of wallpaperswa.com

The Fast-Starting Billionaire

I was a slow starter. I did my best thinking and writing in the morning. But my body needed time to adjust from supine and senseless to vertical and viable. Everything changed when I found an article in Inc. called, "The Habits of Billionaires: 3 Ways to Start Every Day Better". The article targeted three areas: body, mind, and spirit. Since the body plagued me, I attacked it first:

Coming out of bed, your body needs three things for certain — water, protein and movement ... 16 ounces of water gets you started ... You need protein in your first food of the day, even if you are going for a run or a workout ... Movement gets blood moving, clears the mind and releases energy.

Got it. The first day, I jumped up at 6:00 a.m., bolted down to the kitchen, and chugged 16 ounces of water. I immediately learned fighting one's gag reflex is a physical activity and a more strenuous one than I was used to performing so early. Clever.

I grabbed my protein powder, realizing I'd have to mix it with … more water. I shoveled two heaping scoops into another 16 ounces of water, shook the concoction until the powder dissolved, and chugged that. I had to lash my jaw shut with baling wire and put Vise Grips on my lips, but I kept the protein shake down.

Then I headed to the gym. Concerned about keeping 32 ounces of protein-suffused liquid down — and able to breathe only through my nose — I ruled out cardio. I loaded a barbell, reclined under it on the bench, took a deep breath, and … awoke around noon. Refreshed from my nap, I resolved to address my mind:

Your mind needs focus or you will waste time and energy … A billionaire I interviewed told me one of his keys to success — he tries to accomplish only one thing per day. A very big thing, of course, but from the moment he woke up until he finished his day, he threw every available effort at that one thing.

Right. I'd already successfully focused on one thing — keeping my protein shake down. I'd be a billionaire in no time. I removed the Vise Grips from my lips and used wire cutters to snip the baling wire from my jaw. I jogged to the mailbox for my first big check. It wasn't there. But it was imminent. It had to be. I was pumped, primed, and perfectly prepared for perennial prosperity.

Knowing I had it all but made, I grabbed the magazine again to make short work of my spiritual shortcomings. Since the body and mind parts had been duck soup, the spirit thing would be a cinch:

"Being grateful, aware of all you have … starts your day with energy and calm. When you greet your employees, clients, and suppliers throughout the day knowing that you included them in your reflections, they will feel that in your interaction and it will make for a better exchange regardless of the circumstances."

No sweat. I assumed the Lotus position, closed my eyes, concentrated on my breathing, and reflected on my gratitude. It worked. Everyone with whom I came in contact that day shared my gratitude at not honking up that protein shake. I was transformed.

I'm not a billionaire yet. But I'm a new man, a properly awakened man. I've aligned my body, my mind, and my spirit.

And I did it without tossing my cookies.

image courtesy of pixabay.com

You Can Run, But You Can't Hide

You might not be annoyed with Neal Goldman yet. But you will be. When you will be is still up for grabs. But given the pace and inevitability of technological development, it likely won't be long. And the more successful you become, the more annoyed you'll be because Neal's latest brainchild, about which Greg Lindsay wrote an article for Inc. in 2014, came to fruition (relationshipscience.com). In the article — "Relationship Science: Harnessing Big Data for Power Networking" — Lindsay described Goldman's brainchild, a software program for professional networking called Relationship Science (RelSci: God, I love that kind of talk).

The purpose of RelSci is to ensure passé cultural artifacts like privacy, perspicacity, and prudent apposition will be forever relegated to the proverbial scrapheap of history. In a way, it makes a kind of perverse, inevitable sense: If the point of technology is to connect all of us to each other — tangentially and superficially — has Neal Goldman done anything other than ride the wave? Maybe not. Lindsay describes RelSci as:

... an online platform built with profiles drawn from the 1 percent. It's not some free-for-all social network full of selfies and botspam, like Facebook or Twitter. Nor is it LinkedIn, whose metastatic expansion threatens the integrity of the entire system. And unlike net-worth-obsessed virtual clubhouses such as A Small World, RelSci isn't for swapping houses in Gstaad or getting tips on a fabulous butler in Ibiza. In fact, the point of RelSci has nothing to do with expanding your circle of friends. The point is to use the people you do know to find a pathway to the rich and powerful ones you don't.

But beneath the shiny veneer of technology, there are other, less comfortable things afoot. Note the language of Lindsay's concluding sentences: "RelSci has nothing to do with expanding your circle of friends. The point is to use the people you do know to find a pathway to the rich and powerful ones you you don't." Wow. A pathway to the rich and powerful.

Setting aside the obvious — pandering, class envy, the ability to hondel the unsuspecting souls who may have had the good fortune, the ambition, the vision, and/or the committed drive to achieve more than we have — what we have here is a veritably ubiquitous and virtually inescapable invasion of privacy. If you consider your privacy to be anything at all like a property right, RelSci also is, then, a further usurpation of our private property.

I suppose it's all part of chronology, of the inexorable, inevitable evolutionary march toward the Utopian Global Community. And maybe I'm just getting old and, despite my fervent efforts and best intentions, falling into nostalgia, simple-mindedness, and anachronism. But it's hard not to miss the past when one imagines where we're headed ... and longs for what we're losing.

The existence of RelSci also says something about as individuals. It's an indication of our unwitting immaturity, of what we're willing to tolerate, of the extent to which we blithely concede the integrity of our solitude, what used to be the treasured inviolability of our time and space. Why? Because we think we should?

Some years ago, a friend asked me if I'd like to take LSD with him. With equal parts surprise and resolve, I replied: "Didn't we get past 40 so we wouldn't have to do that anymore? Haven't we earned satisfied curiosities? Thank you. I'm good." (Historical note: That friend is now dead. He took his own life in 2005. See "The Big Why".)

Likewise, I wish for a point in our lives, in our careers — in our arcs toward becoming rich and powerful, regardless of how we define those terms — at which we choose not to be the targets of those who seek to gain by us. I'd like to imagine that part of our respective definitions of rich and powerful might be the occupation of positions above the fray of shameless huckstering, beyond which we might choose and be able to be other than, more than, mere connections on an online platform.

Our seeming inability to escape the ever-lengthening tentacles of so-called disrupting technology recalls an admonition from one of my favorite philosophers: Joe Louis. While he's credited with a few variations on the phrase that follows on a number of occasions, the one for which I remember his using it was his 1946 rematch with Billy Conn.

Louis, the heavyweight champion, had defeated Conn in 1941, knocking him out in the thirteenth round after being out-boxed for the first twelve. They scheduled their rematch after both of them completed their military service in World War II. In response to a comment that the fleeter-of-foot Conn, a natural light heavyweight, might attempt to evade Louis in the ring, Louis said: "He can run, but he can't hide." He was right. He knocked Conn out in the eighth.

As you might recall, I'm no fan of disconnecting. (See "Trust Yourself".) But that doesn't make me a proponent of intrusion. Neal Goldman's platform is just another way — in a seemingly unending proliferation of ways — in which whatever success we might achieve will make us targets for imposition. Whether it's the Fed or the frivolous, we're on the radar and under the microscope.

If you think peace and privacy are hard to come by now, you ain't seen nothin' yet.

photo courtesy of Wikimedia Commons

I Wonder

Years ago, returning from a Sunday afternoon outing with some friends in their station wagon, I said I couldn't believe the weekend was ending — the next day would be Monday already. The three-year-old daughter of my friends called to her father from the wayback, "Daddy, where do the days of the week live?"

That remains my all-time favorite question, as profound as it is full of the singular wonder of children.

Her dad replied softly, "I don't know, Sweetheart." Her mother and I pondered the joy and genius of the question.

It's ironic: In business, we're compelled to talk, write, read, and hear about innovation, invention, and ingenuity. We're bombarded with superlatives — biggest, fastest, greatest, best. But none of it contains the sense of wonder that make such expressions genuine, credible, persuasive, and contagious. Why do we settle so?

Why do we bind ourselves to futures of unconvincing rhetoric and going through motions? Is it really that difficult to find reasons to marvel — to find opportunities to refresh, re-invent, and re-invest in our joy and genius? The answer is no ... but there needs to be purposeful deliberateness about the effort to retain perspectives of wonder.

In 2005, Paul Orfalea, the founder of Kinko's, was the subject of a feature in Fortune Small Business. Orfalea said this, in part:

It's pretty popular among chief executives to ... get to the office at 7 a.m., eat lunch at their desks, and don't leave until well into the evening ... When do they ever have time to sit back and think? Or wander or wonder? ... leaving headquarters got me away from the mundane, daily grind that left no space for insight, inspiration, or innovation. Instead of 'chief executive,' I preferred the title of 'chief wanderer'.

Wonder and wander. That's what children do. It's what their natures compel them to do — untainted; uninhibited; not yet self-conscious; not yet aware of being judged or conditioned to being criticized; not aware of limitations, imposed by the predispositions of others, that translate into self-limiting insecurity and lack of faith. The world is the playground of their curiosity. And their curiosity is boundless. What happened to ours?

A rock pile ceases to be a rock pile the moment a single man contemplates it, bearing within him the image of a cathedral. (Antoine de Saint-Exupéry)

When's the last time we sought to marvel? When were we last mindful of finding at least one thing that struck us as full of wonder? What would it take to amaze us? If we don't know, we have to find it. If we do know, and we can't find it in what we're doing now, we have to make a change.

Exceptions prove rules, and rules were made to be broken. Do something different. Do one thing — anything — differently. It might be your last chance. You can't know till you try.

As an added bonus, you just might discover where the days of the week live.

image courtesy of squidoo.com

Everybody's Got a Story, Kid

In the early- to mid '80s, my former father-in-law, Ed, gave me an opportunity to work in the parking lot he operated in downtown Hartford, Connecticut. I was in my early 30s, a full-time college student, and married to Ed's daughter, with two sons and precious little time for a job. So, I'd tend the parking lot on Friday and Saturday nights. Ed would get some much-needed time off. And I'd pick up a much-needed buck or two.

A working-class guy with no formal education beyond high school, Ed was the closest thing to a philosopher I've ever known. As innately intelligent as he was street-smart, his worldview was informed by a curious intellect; a keen, sympathetic eye for the myriad vagaries of the human condition; an unflagging sense of humor; and a singularly generous spirit. I admired him for all of that. But I love him because he called me

Kid until he passed away in 2019.

Three more things about Ed: (1) He was a great storyteller. (2) The only other person who could make me laugh as hard and as frequently as Ed did is my next younger brother, Keith. And (3) Ed was a cigar smoker. When he took the cigar out of his mouth to talk — holding it between his right thumb and index finger as he waggled the ashes off the tip with the other fingers of his right hand — it added an oddly comic touch, however unwitting or unintended.

On one particularly busy Friday night, Ed stayed for a while to make sure we managed all the traffic coming into the lot. After things quieted down a bit, we walked out to the sidewalk. I stood at the curb as Ed wandered idly west up Asylum Street.

As he walked west, a woman walked east. Her name was Peggy. Not quite destitute, she lived in a tiny apartment on Asylum Hill. Not quite crazy, as far as I could tell, she claimed to have been married to a philosophy professor at a prominent university until hard luck, hard times, and a harder life claimed her. I never knew how much of what she told of her past was true, if any. But I was certain of the challenges in her present.

As they passed each other on the sidewalk, I saw the fingers of Ed's right hand reach subtly out, seeming to brush Peggy's. They didn't appear to otherwise acknowledge each other. They continued walking in opposite directions. As Peggy approached me, she said hello and kept on walking.

When Ed turned to come back toward where I was standing, he realized I'd witnessed what happened. As he walked past me and back into the parking lot, in much the same way Peggy had passed me just seconds before, and without breaking stride, he took his cigar out of his mouth and said this, which is all he ever said on the subject of what I saw, "Everybody's got a story, Kid. Everybody's got a fuckin' story."

The next day was Saturday. My former brother-in-law, Pat, had worked the parking lot for some small event at what was then the Hartford Civic Center that afternoon. I went to relieve him in the evening.

When I got there, I said, "Pat, this is none of my business. So, please feel free to tell me exactly that. But ...." And I told him what I just told you.

Pat gave me a slight, knowing smile, with an almost imperceptible shake of his head, and said, "Yeah, he was probably just slipping her a $20 or a $50. He's been helping her out for years." And therein lies the lesson.

At 18, Ed was in Korea. One night, as he and his fellow GIs slept in the foxhole they'd dug, there was a concussion and a flash. Ed regained consciousness the next morning to find everyone around him dead. Dazed, confused, and very young, he started trudging through the Korean winter, having no idea of direction or destination.

As evidence of his charmed life, the first people he came upon were Americans. They recognized the extent to which he'd been traumatized and started the processing that would put him back in the United States. He arrived in his hometown on a bus, disembarking with no job, no prospects, no one with whom to share his wartime experience, and no more sense of direction than he'd had leaving the foxhole in Korea. A friend gave him a job tending bar in town. Ed took the job and reclaimed himself, his compassion, his sympathy, and his generosity.

Ed shared his Korea story with me just one time, as we shared a night of heavy, cathartic drinking. But I witnessed many more manifestations of the lessons it instilled in him:

If a person came in to park and wanted special care taken with his car, Ed never asked why or said no. He'd take the car, hold the person's keys, and make sure the car was parked safely.

If a street person came into the lot and asked for money, Ed would ask, "Do you want to work for it?" If the person said yes, Ed would hand him a broom and send him down to the garage beneath the lot to sweep up. When the person came back up, and without checking his work, Ed would thank him for his efforts and hand him $10 or $20. And on the stories go.

The value of what Ed gave me has nothing to do with dollars and cents. By his example, he taught me the value of decency, of compassion, of kindness, of respect, of nobility, of modesty, and of putting the stories of others before our own, regardless of how hideous and painful our own stories might be.

If you're ever on the fence about whether you should extend yourself to someone else, just remember this:

Everybody's got a story, Kid. Everybody's got a fuckin' story.

image courtesy of unsplash.com

Danny Gatton: The Darkness of Talent

On October 4, 1994, guitarist Danny Gatton was found dead of a self-inflicted gunshot wound at his home in Newberg, Maryland.

In early 1989, some friends and I had the privilege of seeing and hearing Danny Gatton play in Hartford, Connecticut. It was a cold, snowy Friday night. Danny and his band had played in New York City the night before. The weather had kept them there longer than they'd planned. As a result of their late departure from New York and the treacherous congestion on the Connecticut Turnpike, they arrived in Hartford an hour or so after the show was supposed to have started.

No one who'd braved the storm to see them had left by the time Danny and the band reached the Summit Hotel. After briefly sizing the place up, the four men carried in their own equipment and set it up in the claustrophobic lounge. No fanfare. No roadies. No glamour. No pretense. No supper. No complaints.

After a cursory tuning and no introduction, Danny turned to his bandmates and said the name of a song (we didn't need to hear it), the structure of which his rhythm section might loosely follow for the next three to fifteen minutes or more — or for as long as Danny might happen to be in the thrall of any particular muse. It didn't matter. After counting off time, Danny ascended on the first of the evening's innumerable flights of brilliant, beautiful, breath-stealing improvisation.

If there was a song-list for the performance, it was never relevant in the slightest. Each selection had a beginning. We knew that because we heard Danny count. Some even had lyrics, so those compelled to measure structure in linguistic coherence might be comforted. Aside from those two concessions to convention, the balance of the performance was a cross-section of Danny Gatton's aural and technical imagination, a thrill-packed sluicing of the unbridled musical conduit he was.

After the show, we approached Danny at the bar, fully expecting to find him with little friendliness and less time — tired, hungry, probably sullen, and ready to be left alone. We were wrong. Danny was affable and unassuming, perhaps unknowing of the enormity of his talent and what it would cost in the end, perhaps knowing full well and grateful for the distraction we provided. In any case, he was casual and talkative, comfortable with us, as all strangers are in the common need of the barroom.

I asked him only one question: "With talent like that, how come no one knows about you?"

Danny laughed without bitterness and gave only one answer: "Nobody understands this shit."

By "this shit", Danny meant the talent, the stylistic stew that defied categorization and, so, resisted pigeon-hole approaches to branding him as a commoditized type by those who presumed responsibility for marketing his music. ("He's country. No, he's rockabilly. No, he's jazz", etc.) I continue to be haunted at wondering if Danny knew then how frighteningly and tragically right he was. Except for the initiated — his die-hard, see-him-perform-at-all-costs fans — nobody did understand. Least of all, perhaps, Danny.

Danny Gatton's was a talent as rare, accidental, and dark as any talent given without the capacity to comprehend it. His myth will hold that he was playing by age two and that, by age ten, several instructors had advised Daniel (Sr.) and Norma Gatton to save the money they were spending for their son's lessons. Danny couldn't and didn't need to be taught — he was capable of simply hearing something once and playing it.

For embellishment, he was able to translate the wanderings of his imagination into the free-fall of his fretboard explorations. Un-asked-for and never understood, Danny Gatton's enormous talent existed, for him, to be coped with.

Obvious comparisons obtain — Jimi Hendrix, Janis Joplin, Jim Morrison, Mike Bloomfield, et al. — musicians and chronological peers of Danny Gatton, victims of their own hands and talents, however inadvertently or indirectly. But a non-musical personality, whose fate was determined just a year after Danny's, offers a further, darker, and more instructive parallel: O.J. Simpson.

Like Danny Gatton, The Juice was possessed of a talent arguably bigger than he was. He was given the ability to carry a ball with uncanny grace, speed, and style, fleetly eluding big men who tried to maim him as he did so. He ran surely, instinctively, eyes darting and feet moving to the arcane rhythms of his heart and soul. Some of those rhythms were athletic. Some, it continues to be alleged, were not.

Likewise, Danny Gatton played guitar with inimitable inventiveness and boundless abandon, deliberately eluding big men who tried to classify, package, market, and sell him as he did so, deftly picking and fretting the sweet strains of melody and the spasms of dissonance that moved him.

To hear that melodic sweetness and manic dissonance, listen to the Jackie Gleason composition, "Melancholy Serenade", from the 1987 album, ironically entitled, *Unfinished Business.*

Danny Gatton played surely, intuitively, eyes closing and fingers flying to the arcane rhythms of his heart and soul. Some of those rhythms were musical. Some, we now know sadly, were not.

Both these gifted men lived with and within packaging machines, professional people determined and processes intended to make them appear to be beings they were not, to make the two of them marketable, likable, bankable commodities for the bigger commercial interests that sought to control and profit by them. Neither was what he was trying to be made to be; neither was ultimately manipulable.

The Juice was never an affable celebrity, basking in the life-long afterglow of athletic success. He was seething, jealous insecurity, apparently waiting to erupt in the absence of having known himself. Danny was never a one-style wonder, blithely branded and blissfully bound by the marketing types who would otherwise have steered him numbly and narrowly toward their own visions and versions of success. He was silently suffering insecurity, tragically waiting to end the commercial world's inability to recognize — and to accept in unfettered fashion — his genius.

Danny Gatton was never predictable, never classifiable by genre or style. (*Guitar Player* magazine's Reader's Poll named him Best Country Guitarist three years running. No one understood that less or suffered for the absurd narrowness of that designation more than Danny.) He was, rather, a husband, father, and antique car collector and mechanic, hoping he and the world could come to terms with the music that found its way through him. Neither man knew contentment. In the end, O.J. Simpson was acquitted of taking the lives of two others. Danny Gatton was convicted of taking his own.

News of Danny's death gave music momentary pause in hushed surprise and futile wonder. Sales of his records peaked modestly. Specialty shops received requests for his handful of independent-label releases. Cut-out bins were raided for *88 Elmira Street* and *Cruisin' Deuces*, the two albums Elektra let him complete before canceling the five remaining on his contract (arguably because they didn't understand that shit). Then interest waned, and so did Danny's brush with posthumous notoriety.

All of that will matter as little as the structure of the songs he performed.

Danny Gatton's gone now; and outside of his family — and a small and ever-shrinking world of guitar-players, music-lovers, and those with the strength to know and have faith in that which they cannot comprehend — he may one day, sadly, be forgotten.

He took with him a talent as dark as light, as pure as curiosity.

image courtesy of amazon.com

Where the Lines Are

Doctor Benjamin Spock's book, *The Common Sense Book of Baby and Child Care*, was first published in 1946. One of its principal tenets is that children crave the knowledge of their limitations. Some parents learn that more quickly than others. Some parents never learn it at all. And sometimes children come to learn it, to the astonishment of their parents.

The older of my two sons, Sean, was born 37 years after the publication of Dr. Spock's book — on October 6, 1983, to be precise. Sixteen years later, he was acting out his adolescent irrationality in myriad ways that included taking his mother's car without her permission, without a driver's license, and frequently without her knowledge. (If you think the fact that he took his mother's car at other times without a license and with his mother's knowledge is even more alarming, trust your instincts.) Sean's mother and I were divorced by then. Because we shared custody of our two sons, she made me aware of what

Sean was doing.

During one of Sean's every-other-weekend stays with me, I told him I was afraid. He asked why. More precisely, he said, "What the hell are you scared about?" I explained my fear of the possibility that his behavior could land him in the proverbial system, in a set of circumstances over which neither of us would have any control. He appeared to listen. But he didn't hear.

On Friday, December 31, 1999, New Year's Eve, Sean, still sans driver's license, attended a party in the neighborhood in West Hartford, Connecticut, in which he lived with his mother. He and a friend (we'll call him Jack), who was not yet 16, decided to leave the party early. Both of them were aware that another friend, a boy Sean had grown up with (we'll call him Junior) had gone away with his family for the weekend. Sean knew how to get into their home through a window they always left unlocked. He knew where Junior's father, an attorney (we'll call him Senior), kept his car keys. He knew the combination to the lock on the garage. He knew how to drive. He didn't know enough not to use any of that knowledge.

Sean and Jack took Senior's car, a Volvo sedan, and went for a ride. They cruised around, picked up Jack's girlfriend, impressed a few of their buddies, convinced themselves they were somewhere on the Adolescent Judgment Scale between Cool and

Invincible, and, sometime in the wee hours of Saturday, put the car back, locked the garage, and put the keys back.

Quickly sliding up the Scale to Slick, they deduced, of course, that if they could get away with something once, they could get away with that same something again. Armed with that delusion, they went back to the same family's home again Saturday night. Sean went in again, took Senior's car keys again, unlocked the garage again, and took Senior's car again.

What Sean and Jack couldn't know was that, during his family's weekend getaway, Senior remembered he had an obligation to fulfill on Sunday, requiring his return on Saturday night. When Sean and Jack drove into the neighborhood to return Senior's car, they were horrified to find the family van in the driveway, all the lights in the house on — including the floodlights that illuminated the driveway — and the family busily unloading the van.

Their addled adolescent minds notwithstanding, Sean and Jack had presence of mind enough to panic. They drove past the house and escaped notice, even as they feverishly plotted Plan B, which they ended up with no time to formulate: Shortly after getting into the house, Senior noticed the keys to his Volvo were missing. He noticed the Volvo was missing. He called the phone that was in the car. When it rang, Sean and Jack went from panicked to freaked.

Heading north out of the neighborhood, they reached Albany Avenue. Heading east on Albany Avenue, they crossed the city line into Hartford and, more specifically, into the city's notorious and very dangerous North End. Sean then hung a quick left on Mark Twain Drive and veered right into a housing project on Dillon Road. He and Jack bailed out of the car. Sean tossed the keys into a dumpster, and both of them managed to hoof it out of the projects and the North End without becoming body-count statistics.

In January of 2000, I was working at a small public-relations agency in Avon, Connecticut. One night during the middle of the month, I was in my office much later than I should have been. The phone on my desk rang. It was Senior. The call went like this:

Senior: Hi, Mark. It's Senior.

Me: Hi! How are you? Happy New Year.

Senior: Can you meet me at the Hartford Police Station?

Me: Sure. When?

Senior: Now. I'm here with Sean and Jack.

Me: What happened?

Senior: Just get here.

When I arrived at HPD, Senior looked to be some combination of peeved and crestfallen. The desk sergeant looked to be some combination of bored and curious. Sean and Jack looked to be some combination of mildly concerned and adolescently defiant. Jack's father looked to be some combination of aloof and inconvenienced. The two patrolmen who stood next to the boys looked to be some combination of inured and impatient. I was some combination of angry, disappointed, and terrified.

Senior said to Jack's father and me, "The boys will get into a cruiser with the officers. They'll give the officers directions to where they left my car. I'll drive behind them. You'll drive behind me."

There was no hesitation in Senior's voice, no equivocation, no nervous edge. It was certain, authoritative, and direct. It neither invited nor permitted questioning. The desk sergeant and the patrolmen said nothing. Neither did anyone else.

Four cars drove slowly through the dark in a cold January rain, made colder by the dank chill of the procession's mission — north on High Street, west on Albany Avenue, north on Mark Twain Drive, east on Dillon Road. The Volvo sat where Sean and Jack had left it, seemingly untouched. Senior, with a second set of keys, opened the driver's side door. The phone was still there.

He opened the trunk. His late father's golf clubs were still there. He breathed a sigh of relief none of the rest of us felt at all.

On the way home that night, I was crying. "Why the hell are YOU crying?" Sean asked like the teenager he was.

I said, "Remember the conversation in which I told you I was afraid we'd come to a point at which we were in the system and at its mercy? We're there. We have no control. We have no way of predicting what will happen. We have no idea of the prices to be paid. All we can do now is wait."

Sean said, "All I did was borrow a car."

"That's your perspective. From the perspective of the law, you're guilty of driving without a license. That's a misdemeanor. You're also guilty of breaking and entering, plus grand theft auto. Those are felonies. And the only difference between you and Vince [a friend of Sean who was doing time for his own felony conviction] is whatever you think of yourself because Vince, obviously, thinks nothing of himself."

The next day, Senior called me. He explained how he'd learned what happened to his car, who did it, and where it was. He told me Jack's girlfriend, miffed over some perceived slight, had called to tell him the story, two weeks after the fact. He told me he believed Sean needed to be taught a lesson. I told him he was right, and I was ready to face the music with him.

Because Senior's an attorney, he knew there were two jurisdictions involved — West Hartford, whence his car had been stolen, and Hartford, the jurisdiction in which it had been recovered. He told me he was going to press charges in West Hartford, but not in Hartford, since Sean's time in the system would be considerably more brutal in Hartford, at least in part because of the fact that he might be detained in the infamous Morgan Street lock-up. I thanked Senior for that consideration.

I took Sean to his appointment to be booked on his charges at the West Hartford Police Department. When we arrived, the desk sergeant signed us in, pointed toward a waiting area, and told us to have a seat.

After giving us a few carefully calculated minutes to stew in anxious anticipation, the booking officer came in. "Sean O'Brien!" We both stood up. The officer pointed at me and said, "Not you." I sat down. The officer led Sean away.

When Sean returned, the ink stains still on his fingertips from having his prints taken, he was green. I asked him what was wrong. He told me the officer had taken him through the lock-up on the way to the booking room. I asked Sean, "What got to you, the stuff you saw in there?"

He said, "No ... the smell."

I said a silent prayer of gratitude for the booking officer's savvy.

I retained a defense attorney. I scheduled appointments for Sean and me to attend counseling sessions with a family therapist. I went with Sean to meet with the vice-principal at Northwest Catholic High School, which Sean attended, for which he played basketball, and from which he'd be suspended for two weeks while the administration decided whether to expel him permanently. Subsequent to that, I took Sean to every one of his court dates.

Lest you fear a disastrous ending to this story, fear not: The result of all the ensuing proceedings is that four things saved Sean: First, Senior wrote a letter to the judge who presided over Sean's case. In the letter, which the judge read aloud in court, Senior said he'd known Sean his whole life. He believed him to be a good kid who'd made a bad decision. And he asked the judge for leniency.

Second, Sean was granted first-offender status and was deemed qualified for Accelerated Rehabilitation, the one and only get-out-of-jail-free card to which one is entitled from the State of Connecticut. The two-year-jail term to which Sean otherwise would have been sentenced was suspended. He was given 100 hours of community service.

Third, Sean elected to do his community service at a Salvation Army soup kitchen in downtown Hartford. He could have chosen to sit on his ass in the West Hartford Public Library for 100 hours. He didn't. He opted to see what reality is like if you've drawn fewer advantages from the deck of life than he did.

Fourth, Sean found the sense of himself that his friend, Vince, lacked. He recognized and was grateful for all of the people who'd stood by him and all of the institutions that were willing to believe in him and forgive him. He recognized and was grateful for all the things in his life that the lives of so many others don't and never will have. He may not have come to believe he deserved any of that faith and good fortune just then. But he did understand he had responsibility to continue to earn and uphold it.

Sean turned 38 in October of 2021. He's a good man; a good husband to his wife, Lauren, whose gentle, thoughtful nature he respects and admires; a good father to two children, Evan and Maia; a dedicated employee; and a born basketball coach. He has a keenly developed and hard-earned sense of right and wrong. And he's less quick to question or judge me when I cry, especially when I cry for joy at the man he's become.

When I was a boy of 14, my father was so ignorant I could hardly stand to have the old man around. But when I got to be 21,

I was astonished at how much the old man had learned in seven years." (Mark Twain)

Some years after the incident, I was sitting with Sean, in all likelihood watching a basketball game. I don't know why that New Year's Eve and its ensuing travails crossed my mind. But they did. I said, "Remember the incident with Senior's car?"

"Of course, I do."

"I don't even know if there's an answer to this question. But what the hell, if anything, were you thinking."

Sean said, without a second's hesitation, "I needed to know where the lines were."

Sean didn't then and doesn't now know the first thing about Dr. Spock and his book. But he knew he needed to know his limitations. He needed to know where the lines are. God bless him for knowing.

We all need to know where the lines are.

The New Revised and Enlarged
Edition of His Famous Book

Dr. Benjamin
SPOCK

The Common Sense Book
of Baby and Child Care

image courtesy of ebay.com

The Scale of Reactive Behavioral Modes

I have two younger brothers. The younger of the two, Woody, is already famous. (See "Not So Instant Karma".) He's six years younger than I am. The one in between us, Keith, is a year-and-a-half younger than I am, my Irish twin, if you will. (See "Family Traditions".)

A volatile amalgam of the most belligerently emotional and political predilections — and the most imposing physical characteristics — of Archie Bunker, Paul Bunyan, and Ted "The Mad Stork" Hendricks, Keith is also one of the most hilarious people I know ... as long as you're on his good side. If not, well, Richard Kuklinski could have given Keith anger-management counseling.

The subject of Keith came up when I was working with my friend, Kevin Hinchey, writer and co-director of the documentary film, *Love, Work and Knowledge: The Life and Trials of Wilhelm Reich*. While trying to schedule a Hartford premier for the film, Kevin and I were being put through the King-Size Wringer by the co-executive directors (their self-granted titles) of a theater that describes itself thusly (key identifiers withheld to protect the hapless):

A classic movie palace located on the campus of [snip] in Hartford, Connecticut ... a not-for-profit independent film theater with a magnificent single-screen venue, 485 seats, and a much loved balcony. Built in 1935 ... with a signature design by McKim, Mead and White, [snip] stands to this day as one of the most highly regarded art house cinemas in the country.

If you get the sense that the place (and its co-executive directors) are a tad snooty and take themselves quite seriously, you'd be uncannily correct.

At any rate, after one particularly pernicious working-over, Kevin and I were comparing notes and licking our psychic wounds from the excruciatingly frustrating encounter. I wanted to be able to communicate to Kevin the mixed emotions I was feeling, along with my uncertainty as to how I would react to the co-executive directors.

Since Kevin had never met Keith, I thought a visual aid (as we say in the biz) might be helpful in conveying the range of behavioral responses I was contemplating. So, I created the Scale of Reactive Behavioral Modes that appears with this story.

To help you comprehend the nature, substance, and potential of each of the modes in the scale, I'll explicate them here:

Standby. This is a state of mind and emotions comparable to a holding pattern. With no meaningful stimuli, you're just sort of hanging around, waiting for something to happen before determining how you might react to something — or nothing — if at all.

Limbo. As opposed to a holding pattern, limbo is more like a holding cell. It's Purgatory. It's the place between Heaven and Hell, in which you've experienced enough negative stimuli to feel inclined to react in some way. But since there's still a shred of hope for some positive eventuality, you can't really go anywhere or do anything yet.

Seething. In this mode, you're royally pissed. You know you're highly likely to do something retaliatory. But you haven't gone off yet. And there's still a modicum of possibility that your reaction, whatever it is, might be reasonable ... or, at least, non-lethal.

Keith. This is the proverbial Nuclear Option. It's Hell. It's shock and awe. There's no game plan. There's no possibility for anything mitigating or reasonable. There's no escaping or hiding. There's no getting around a direct hit, along with considerable collateral carnage. The likelihood of casualties is high. The likelihood of survivors is negligible. This is full-on Keith. God help us.

Since it's not likely, dear readers, that any of you might know Keith, all of this will, no doubt, strike you as exaggeration. It's not.

Some years ago, my father went into a local pizza joint to pick up the order he'd phoned in a little while before. Standing at the counter, he saw a dude sitting by himself in a booth toward the back of the dining room. The dude looked like Rocky after coming up on the short end of his first tiff with Apollo Creed. After a few moments, he recognized the dude as Keith. He walked to the back of the room.

"What the hell happened to you."

"I got in a little scrape," Keith replied.

"What does the other guy look like," my father asked, his favorite question when he saw someone who looked as if he might have come up on the short end of anything.

"Not good," Keith said. "And there were five of them."

In the interest of safety — yours — and on the off chance that you cross paths with Keith some time, you might want to print the Scale of Behavioral Modes and keep it in your wallet for handy reference.

Kevin had his laminated.

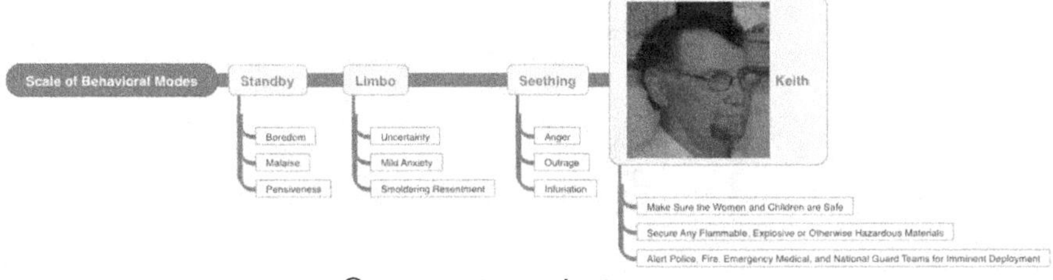

©Mark Nelson O'Brien

My Summer with Chucky

The summers I was 15 and 16, I volunteered at a place that was then called the Regional Training Center Camp (RTCC), adjacent to the grounds of the Powder Ridge ski area in Middlefield, Connecticut. (It's now the John J. Nerden RTC Camp, named for the saint who was its first Executive Director.) The camp was for people of all ages, with all manner of cognitive disabilities. They would arrive by the busload every morning for a full day of activities.

The first summer I was there, I worked in Outdoor Recreation. I got to spend every day in the summer sun, engaging the campers in all the games and outdoor activities in which they might be capable of participating. From softball to basketball, from football to kickball, from hiking to golf, we pretty much did it all. On the days the weather gods were less than pleased, we carried on in the shelter of a large pavilion.

The summer passed pleasantly enough. I enjoyed working with and encouraging the campers. I enjoyed working with and getting to know the other volunteers and the camp's staff members. But I was less than satisfied with the routine. There's just so much creativity and spontaneity you can inject into games comprising one ball and a million rules. I wondered if I'd return to the camp the following summer and, if so, what I'd choose to do.

Knowing the part-time job I'd scored at McDonald's when I turned 16 (see "My First Boss") would afford me the time to return to the camp, I opted to do it. But I asked if I could be placed in something other than Outdoor Rec. I was. I was assigned to a section of the camp referred to as One on One. Every volunteer in that section was assigned to one camper for the entire summer, one camper whose disabilities required individual care every minute of every camping day. I was assigned a boy named Chucky.

Chucky's cognitive challenges were compounded by the fact that he also suffered from cerebral palsy and epilepsy. He was kept sedated to control his seizures. He was confined to a wheelchair. He wore a hockey helmet to protect his head should he fall out of his chair during a seizure or otherwise. He drooled constantly. He had to be fed and watched as he ate, lest he choke. He appeared to be largely unresponsive and was reputed to be non-verbal. That was all I needed.

If you ever want to make sure something gets done, without fail, tell an Irishman he can't do it; that is, tell him he's not capable of doing it or he's not permitted to do it. Conversely, if you ever want to make sure some particular thing never gets done, tell an Irishman he has to do it. Come Hell or high water, I was going to get to that boy if it killed me.

I talked to Chucky deliberately and incessantly from the day we met. I talked to him as if we were peers. I talked to him about whatever was on my mind. I asked him questions. I pretended he was answering me. I'd repeat his imaginary answers aloud, and I'd continue the conversation as if he were holding up his end. I made up and told him ridiculous stories. I did everything but refuse to believe that dull glimmer in his drug-hazed eyes was NOT awareness. Most important, on Day One, I determined to call him Arnold.

One day, in one of the last weeks of the summer, I was carrying on as usual. I laid one of my typical absurdities on him and said, "Right, Arnold?" His face suddenly lit up like the sun. That boy's eyes blazed right through the chemicals that were supposed to keep them dull and unreflective. He broke out in the biggest, goofiest, most life-affirming, heart-filling, and spirit-lifting smile I've ever seen. And he said with unabashed delight, loudly enough so everyone in the building could hear him: "No! Chucky!"

I can't dance a step. God must have thought it would be hilarious to give me two left feet, a near-fatal lack of coordination, and a paralyzing self-consciousness of both. But with everybody in the building headed our way at a gallop, I picked Chucky up out of that chair, held him in my arms, and danced around the building with him, laughing and crying like I'm laughing and crying right now. I still have no idea which one of the two of us was happier. It never mattered.

At the end of that summer, I was awarded a certificate from The Eunice Kennedy Shriver National Institute of Child Health and Human Development (NICHD), signed by Mrs. Shriver, for my work with Chucky. And all I did was help that boy find a way to smile and talk.

So, the next time you're tempted to think you're just one person, that you can't make a difference, that you're invisible, anonymous, powerless, unable, incapable, or anything else equally self-belittling, please remember this story. I do. I always will.

It teaches me the immeasurable power in one boy's smile.

image courtesy of nl.stockfresh.com

I Found All the Polite People

◇

The findings presented here shouldn't be considered in any way scientific. What's more, the evidence compiled herein certainly doesn't constitute a statistically significant sampling. And the story I'm about to relate should positively be considered anecdotal. But all of that notwithstanding, I finally found out where all the polite people ended up: They're working at Dunkin'.

I gathered the results of this decidedly informal survey at three local Dunkin' outlets. By local, I mean in or near South Windsor, Connecticut, the town in which we resided at the time. Since America, after all, runs on Dunkin', geographic specificity is of paramount importance here, no? I visited each of the outlets on three completely separate occasions. The elements common to each of my three orders were a lovely breakfast sandwich (a different one each time) and a large dark-roast coffee now called

Midnight), hot and black. I limited my study to the drive-thru lanes at all of the three outlets.

Outlet #1

This shop is located in close proximity to the salon in which I get my haircut. Since I'd scheduled a recent ears-lowering appointment early enough to compel my getting up before breakfast, I emerged from the salon freshly coiffed, staggeringly handsome, incorrigibly modest, and ravenously hungry.

Spotting Dunkin' across the parking lot, I steered my vehicle (that's vee-HICK-el if you're from the South) toward the entrance of the drive-thru lane, followed the arrows painted on the pavement to the menu board, waited for a disembodied voice to ask me what I wanted, and placed my order. The voice then instructed me to shift my transmission to Drive and to proceed to the pick-up window.

At the window, I was greeted by a young man. He asked me, with obvious sincerity, how I was that fine morning (aside from freshly coiffed, staggeringly handsome, incorrigibly modest, and ravenously hungry). He told me a fresh pot of dark-roast coffee hadn't quite finished brewing yet. But, he went on, if I'd like to take a spot in the parking lot, he'd be happy to bring my coffee out to my car. I thanked him, parked my car, and went inside.

When he saw me enter the shop, the young man approached me and reiterated what he'd told me. I said, "You're hard at work. I'm not. And if you're polite and generous enough to offer to deliver my coffee to me, the least I can do is come in to get it, shake your hand, and thank you for your exemplary service." Then I told his manager what he'd done.

Outlet #2

The next shop I visited happened to be on a fairly busy thoroughfare I was traversing after having helped my wife, Anne, with a residential–staging project. Suddenly recovering from a bout of amnesia, I remembered I'd forgotten to eat breakfast that morning. Spotting the Dunkin' sign to the left in my peripheral vision, I jerked my steering wheel hard to port, veered across two lanes of oncoming traffic, screamed into the parking lot, scared the shit out of a guy who spit out his dentures along with his glazed cruller, locked up my brakes, and did a fishtail skid up to the menu board.

As the smoke from my screeching tires cleared, I heard a disembodied woman's voice say, "Good morning. May I help you?" After I'd placed my order, I was instructed to pull up to the next window. I did. There, I was greeted by a young man, every bit the polite equal of the young man I'd met at my last Dunkin' visit. He, too, asked sincerely how I was that morning. After cheerily taking my money, he instructed me to pull ahead to yet another window, from which my order would be dispensed. I did just that.

A young woman, even more pleasant than the young man I'd just encountered, opened the window. Smiling, she had a bag with my lovely breakfast sandwich in it in her left hand. In her right hand, she held my coffee, freshly poured in one of the new paper cups with which Dunkin' has replaced styrofoam. Before leaning out to hand them to me, she smiled and asked me how I was. I told her I was fine, albeit a little worried about the guy with the cruller. And I asked her how her day was going.

Beaming, she said, "Wonderfully!" She told me the store had given the guy a fresh cruller and that his choppers hadn't broken when they hit the pavement. He just dunked 'em in a fresh cup of coffee, which the store also gave him on the house, and slid them back in his yap. All's well that ends well.

Outlet #3

My research concluded at a Dunkin' that happens to be on a well-traveled secondary road — three lanes in either direction — adjacent to a major shopping mall and the entrances to and exits from two interstate highways, I-84 and I-384. Consequently, the place does a land-office business, day and night, catering to the needs of the traffic-stressed, the shopped-out, the road-weary, and the caffeine-addicted (like yours truly). I pulled into the drive-thru lane, this time with Eddie (our dog) riding shotgun in his doggy seat.

Eddie and I waited for the disembodied voice, this one, again, a young woman's. After placing my order, I followed her obligatory instruction to pull ahead to the window. The same voice, this time in the body of the young woman who owned it, greeted us at the window. Spotting Eddie, her smile got even wider. She said, "Oh, my God. How cute!"

Eddie said, "Don't get your hopes up. She's not talking to you."

I turned my head back toward the young woman hopefully. She looked right past me and asked, "May I give him a Munchkin?"

Crushed but determined not to telegraph my wounded vanity, I said, "No, thank you. He doesn't eat people food."

The Moral of the Story

The bad news is there's no shortage of generalized, generational bad-news stories or people willing to tell them. Baby Boomers this. Generation X that. Millenials the other thing. Generation Z something else. We can stereotype all we want. And we do. In truth and fairness to all of us, every stereotype, like every cliché, has elements of truth in it. That's how they start. And it's why they're perpetuated.

The good news is every stereotype breaks down at the level of the individual. And if we take the time to know people — individual people — we'll find that people are like cats: There are truthful generalizations to be made about every one. But every one is different in personality, in temperament, in its capacities for communicating, for giving, for loving.

That's how I found all the polite people. They work at Dunkin'.

But don't take my word for it. Ask Eddie.

© today.com

I Don't Think We're in Kansas Anymore

One day, while I was living in Westbrook, Connecticut, I took my bike out on a Saturday for a long ride. On the north side of the Baldwin Bridge, the I-95 bridge that crosses the Connecticut River between Old Saybrook and Old Lyme, there's a paved path for pedestrians and cyclists. It's separated from the highway by a concrete barrier. The bridge ascends to a crest in the middle, sloping to either side beyond the crest. Crossing the river, I took Route 156 through Old Lyme. Continuing on, I passed Rocky Neck State Park in East Lyme and the York Correctional Institution in Niantic, crossed the Niantic River into Waterford, and circled back on Route 1, the Boston Post Road, to Old Lyme.

As I was nearing the Baldwin Bridge on the return trip, I noticed storm clouds gathering. The clouds weren't completely unexpected since it was summer. But I didn't anticipate the speed with which the storm would hit.

Ascending the bridge, the wind picked up and there was a light sprinkle. But as I reach the crest heading toward Old Saybrook, Hell broke loose.

The rain exploded in buckets. Lightning flashed. Thunder boomed. And the wind blustered and whirled like the cyclone that took Dorothy to Oz. In what could be fairly characterized as an atomic adrenaline rush, I pedaled as quickly as I could down the remaining length of the bridge onto Essex Road, stood into my pedals as I flew past the American Legion and the Comfort Café, veered into the parking lot of the Quality Inn, and took shelter in the foyer.

The clerk behind the desk in the Inn looked across the lobby to see what the clown in the helmet and the soaking wet spandex might be up to. But he didn't come over to ask. He didn't throw me out. And he didn't call the police.

Someone once asked the legendary golfer, Lee Trevino, what he'd do if he ever got caught in the middle of a golf course in a lightning storm. He said, "I'd hold a 1 iron over my head because not even God can hit a 1 iron."

I don't know if God can hit a frantic cyclist. But on that day crossing the Baldwin Bridge, I chose not to find out.

licensed from clipartof.com

Over My Head

My father loved to take on projects of all kinds — woodworking, landscaping, home-improvement, political. And he had an incorrigible knack for getting in over his head on every one. It's a knack I inherited, at least to some extent. Case in point:

In 2009, Mom and Dad were living in South Carolina. But they'd come to Connecticut for a visit. I was living in Westbrook at the time. On the east side of my property, sandstone ledge rose perhaps 15 to 20 feet before sloping off abruptly to the property next door. At the top of that ledge, growing out horizontally then rising vertically toward the sun, was the trunk of a cherry tree. During some storm or other, the top of that tree had been blown off. But a good 12 to 15 feet of that tree still stood. I don't know why, but I wanted it down. With Dad there, I thought my timing for taking it down was good. I should have known better.

On a Saturday afternoon during their visit, I said to Dad, "Do you think I can cut through that thing with my bow saw?"

"Sure," he said, "Give it a try.

Trusty bow saw in hand, I climbed up the ledge, positioned myself securely, and started to saw. At the point at which I'd sawn far enough into the horizontal part of that tall stump that the bow of my saw met the stump, I could saw no more. As much as I hauled on and hung from what was left of the trunk, it didn't budge. And I was unable to extract my saw from it.

"I'll have to drive to Essex Hardware [an eight-mile round trip] and get a wedge and a striking hammer," I told Dad. He declined to take the ride with me.

On my return, I scaled the ledge again. I placed the wedge into the groove I'd cut with the saw and started pounding. I forced the wedge all the way into the groove until it would go no farther. Nothing happened.

"I'll have to drive to Essex Hardware again and get another wedge and a bigger hammer," I told Dad. He once again declined to take the ride with me.

Coming back hell-bent to take down that stump, I clambered up the ledge. I pounded the second, bigger wedge in as far as I'd driven the first. I hauled on and hung from the trunk again.

Nothing happened.

I got back in my car. I went back to the hardware store. I'm fairly sure the crew in the store was taking bets on how many more times I'd be back. But I didn't ask. And the crew members were good enough not to ask what I was doing or what was wrong with me. I returned from the store with an even bigger wedge and a sledgehammer. I set the wedge and wailed on it for all I was worth. When I finally heard the cracking sound I'd been waiting for all afternoon, I warned Dad to stand clear of the ledge. After a few more strikes of the hammer, the stump broke free and tumbled down the ledge. Whew.

I had one of those eight-cubic-foot wheelbarrows with the two inflatable front tires. I got that out. With Dad's help, we balanced the 12 or 15 feet of the stump across the wheelbarrow and managed to get it down to the front part of the yard where the landscaper typically left the junk he'd pick up on his next trip by with a truck.

On Monday afternoon, my doorbell rang. It was a young man from the landscaping service.

"Hi, Mark. Can I borrow your chainsaw? I want to cut up that cherry trunk, so I can put it in the truck."

"I don't have a chainsaw," I replied.

Looking at me in astonishment, he asked, "How'd you get that cherry trunk down?"

"Don't ask," I said. "You'd have to know my dad. Do you want a hand humping it into the truck?"

"Sure," he said.

The stump was gone. My predilection for getting in over my head was not.

image courtesy of pixabay.com

This, Too, Shall Pass

In 1987, my friend and co-worker at The Travelers Insurance Company, Rick Lovallo, and I went to Toad's Place in New Haven, Connecticut, to see the guitarist, Robin Trower. Robin was touring in support of the album he'd released earlier that year, *Passion*. Given the shortage of parking on York Street, Elm Street, or Broadway — and since we were too cheap to pay for parking — we parked in the lot of Yale University's Payne Whitney Gym, farther up York Street at the intersection of Tower Parkway.

Robin put on his typically mesmerizing performance. As we were leaving Toad's Place, all I can remember Rick saying to me was, "Wow, man. He's a really heavy cat."

When we stepped out onto York Street, it was pouring rain. We, of course, hadn't brought umbrellas or worn raincoats. So, we decided to run back to the parking lot in an effort to minimize the soaking we were going to get anyway. We arrived at my car winded and wet but nonetheless happy to have reached shelter and warmth. On the way back to Hartford, we chatted rather aimlessly about all manner of things, including the show we'd just seen, work, and whatever else might have crossed our minds.

At the time, we both worked for a gentleman named Len Kendall. Len always referred to Rick as The Inspector, given Rick's resemblance — in his facial appearance, the mustache he had at the time, and the hat and the trench coat he favored — to the Peter Sellers character, Inspector Clouseau, from the Pink Panther films. The morning following the Robin Trower concert, Len stuck his head in my cubicle.

"Where's The Inspector?"

"I don't know," I answered. "I went to a show in New Haven with him last night, and he was fine."

Len and I might have thought about it periodically during the day. But given the dependable employee we knew Rick to be, we didn't worry too much. But Rick didn't show up the next day, either. At that point, Len and I were concerned enough that Len called Rick's home. Rick's wife answered the phone.

It turned out that in our run to the car two nights before, Rick had shaken loose a kidney stone he never knew he had. To say he was in agony would be an understatement. And to engage in too much detail about what he endured thereafter would be indelicate.

Suffice it to say the stone passed. He never had another one. And we've gone on to see innumerable shows since then without incident.

image courtesy of pixabay.com

Happy Meal

I recently stopped in a coffee shop for lunch. As I was paying for my repast, the earnest young man behind the counter told me all the food was prepared on the premises and said proudly, "It's all food you can feel good about eating."

Uh oh. Had I been neglecting to feel bad about what I eat? Was I missing an opportunity to feel guilty or to diminish my self-esteem for following my own gustatory groove? The next time I'm savoring a meal, will I blow the chance to double my pleasure by failing to beat myself up over my own enjoyment?

The young man surely meant well and intended no slight. But that kind of unwitting happy-making may not have been the boost for his brand he imagined. It suggests we may finally have lost ALL of our marbles, kids.

To feel good about eating, we apparently have to eat fresh, locally sourced, organic foods only. If we do, we'll live forever, of course. But don't worry: There'll be room for all of us around the campfire.

We will, though, have to overlook the fact that the science we now deem bad made it possible to feed mass populations and free entire societies from what used to be considered plagues. And we'll have to ignore the fact that mass-farming techniques made it possible to produce more food at less cost.

Oh, we'll also have to forget that the same folks who have their knickers in a twist over GMOs, processed and frozen foods, and anything else we shouldn't feel good about eating are the same folks who decry diminishing global food supplies and escalating global food prices. But nobody said it would be easy. Heck, even Kermit the Frog knows it's not easy being green.

I'm all for healthy dietary choices and supporting local merchants. But I'm also for practicality. So, what if we just relaxed? What if we separated ideology from ingestion and left each other to our own preferences? What if we assumed the other guy knows what he's doing and feels good about it? What if we don't assume he needs to hear what we think we should tell him? What if we just enjoy our tofu and bean sprouts in silence and let the other guy enjoy his Big Mac in peace?

If we managed to do those things — if we steered clear of such prandial proselytizing and left each other to our own pantophagous preferences — maybe we'd manage to enjoy ourselves a little more and worry a little less.

Dude. Are you gonna eat those fries?

image courtesy of pixabay.com

Pay it Forward

In the late summer of 2006, I was a novice cyclist. I lived in Middletown, Connecticut, at the time. (See "Family Traditions".) Early one evening, I headed out for a ride. I made my way west through Middlefield into Meriden, my hometown, and across to the Chamberlain Highway on Meriden's west side. I intended to ride north through Kensington, then east through Berlin and East Berlin, and back into Middletown by way of Cromwell. Intended.

Less than a half-mile up the Chamberlain Highway, my rear tire went flat. I panicked momentarily. Then I collected my wits and took inventory. I had a spare tube, along with the CO_2 cartridge required to inflate it and the CO_2 gun to fit over the valve in the new tube, thereby permitting the pressurized CO_2 to flow into the new tube. I also had my inexperience.

As a result of that inexperience, I'd neglected to note the hour of my departure, the fact that it would be dark by the time I got home, and to bring my trifocals. I wore only non-prescription sunglasses. Though I managed to get the rear wheel off, I soon realized the dimming light, the dark lenses I wore, and my blurred vision would make the rest of the job dicey.

Sure enough. After I'd managed to get the tire off the rim, the old tube out, and the new tube in, largely by feel, it came time to inflate the new tube. I put the CO_2 cartridge into the gun, got the gun over the valve as well as I could, and pulled the trigger: PPPPFFFFTTTTT!!!!

The gun was empty. The tube was still flat.

Swearing loudly (there was no one there to hear) and pulling my phone from the pouch under my saddle, I called my brother, Keith, who lived in Meriden at the time. No answer. I lived alone. I had no one else to call.

It was official. I was stranded.

As I sat in the grass on the side of the road, facing north and wondering what the hell I was going to do, I became aware of brightening lights illuminating the scene from the south. As I looked up, a van pulled to the side of the road. The passenger window slid down. The woman in the driver's seat said, "Do you need help?

I got up, approached the van, rested my elbows on the door, and peered in. I said, "I'm stuck here." I told her the story and where I lived.

"Do you want a ride home? We're headed home, too, and we live right in East Berlin."

I looked left into the back seat of the van. Two young boys were strapped in car seats, each playing a video game.

"You don't even know me," I said. "You have no reason to believe you can trust me with you or your sons. Doesn't that strike you as potentially dangerous?"

"You have an honest face. You have a trustworthy voice. And I'm going to call my husband and let him know what I'm doing and where we're going."

"Please call him before I get in. If he's okay with your giving me a ride, please keep him on the line. I'd like him to know you're safe the entire way, and I'd like to be able to speak with him."

She did. I threw my bike in the back of her van. I told her my name. She told me her name was Suzanne, and we headed for Middletown, both of us talking with her husband the whole way.

When we arrived at my home, I pulled my bike out of Suzanne's van and asked her to wait a moment while I ran in to get a business card. Coming back out with the card, I handed it to her and said, "All of my contact information is on here. If there's ever anything I can do for you or your husband to repay your kindness — anything — please don't hesitate for a moment to let me know."

With a gentle smile, Suzanne said only, "Pay it forward."

Then she, her sons, and their van dissolved into the night like Big Joe and Phantom 309.

(Please look up Tom Waits, Big Joe and Phantom 309, on YouTube. Play the version that's seven minutes and 12 seconds long.)

image courtesy of behance.net

Not So Instant Karma

In the past, we'd have said the younger of my two younger brothers, Woody,* is mentally retarded. In these enlightened times, we're more likely to say he's intellectually disadvantaged, synaptically challenged, cognitively attenuated, neuronally insufficient, operating at an electroencephalogramitcal deficit, or something equally nebulous and faux-scientific to virtue-signal our sensitivity and to ensure our compliance with the inviolable laws of political correctness.

All such linguistic nonsense is just euphemistic bet-hedging. We're merely trying not to acknowledge that Woody's challenges make him in some ways more perceptive, in many ways more imaginative, and in all ways much more capable of simplifying than we are. An example:

One evening, after a phone conversation with Woody, I wrote these notes to myself:

Tonight, Woody told me he and some friends from his group home were going to Europe for a vacation. At first, I disbelieved him. But when he said they were going to "Spain, Germany, and all those other French countries down there" — and that they would also visit Arkansas — I was ashamed of myself for doubting. This is not a matter of geographic facility. It's a question of imagination. Woody's is better than mine. That's why I'm the writer.

He's also more patient, caring, and capable of tending his convictions without doubt than we are. Someone once told me the measure of a practical joker is that he need not witness the payoff of his jokes. Likewise, the measure of a sense of karma is that one need not witness the turning of the wheel to know what's right, to know what deserves constancy. Another example:

Every visit to the house Woody shares with two roommates (under 24/7 supervision) requires a visit to his bedroom. An avid collector of model airplanes, CDs, stuffed animals, professional wrestling DVDs and posters, radio scanners, and family pictures, Woody's always eager to share his new prize possessions with anyone willing and able to slow down and simplify enough to appreciate them.

On one such visit, I was looking up at the new planes that hung on nearly invisible fishing line from his ceiling. Puffs of cotton clouds, also suspended on fishing line, floated among them. Interspersed between the planes and the clouds, glow-in-the-dark stars twinkled in the dimming light of early evening. As I was gazing, Woody said, "What do I do with that?"

I looked down in the direction he was pointing. "That" was a 13-gallon trashcan, filled to the brim with aluminum pull-tabs from soda and beer cans. As I tried to fathom the time and diligence required to amass such a collection, I could only think to ask, "Why did you save all those?"

Woody said, "Frank told me to."

Frank was a cousin of my mother. He passed away in May of 1996. Woody explained to me that, at one of the traditional Christmas Eve parties Frank and his wife threw every year, tending bar as he always did and sporting his holly bow tie, Frank told Woody if he saved the tabs from aluminum cans, some charitable organization could redeem them and use the funds to help someone. Woody neither forgot nor wavered.

As I stood, awestruck at the enormity of what Woody had accomplished, all I could manage to say was, "I have no idea."

Shortly thereafter, I received a call from a woman in the organization that manages Woody's residence. She asked my permission to give Woody's name to the Shriners of Connecticut. Through some connections he'd made, Woody found a way to donate the tabs to the Shriners, who redeemed them and used the proceeds for their Hospitals for Children. The Shriners were so moved by how many tabs Woody collected, at how long he'd stayed his course, they wanted to write him a letter and send him a plaque.

And so it is that the next time you visit Woody's room, you'll see that plaque proudly displayed on his wall. He was lucky enough to see the wheel turn. But he didn't need to. And he won't need to see it turn again, even though it surely will.

While you're there, you'll also see that trashcan is nearly full again. And if you believe in karma, you'll become one of the many friends and family members who save tabs and send them to Woody from all over the country.

In the midst of all the world's talk about making a difference, Woody says nothing. He just stays his course.

Instant karma? Woody doesn't need it. In the midst of his ostensible challenges, he's content with imagination, a full heart, a just reward, and continuing his mission.

Frank told him to.

* Woody is a nickname derived from Hollywood. My father once put an old pair of tortoise-shell sunglasses in the junk drawer every kitchen is required to have by law. Woody pulled them out one day and put them on. My father saw him sporting those shades and called him Mister Hollywood. The rest, as they say ....

image courtesy of support.shrinershospitals.org

Tell the Truth

All you have to do is write one true sentence. Write the truest sentence that you know. (Ernest Hemingway, A Moveable Feast)

When I first began presenting the first book I wrote for children, Martin the Marlin, to large groups of young students, I'd find myself getting anxious. Oddly enough, I wasn't concerned about what the teachers might think of what I had to say. I was worried about how I'd relate to the children — and how they'd relate to me. Then I remembered two things:

First, I remembered, as a child, wishing adults would tell me the truth ... about anything ... about everything. I knew I could handle it. I was less sure about the adults. But that never got to be an issue, since they seemed to scrutinize — then soften, sugarcoat, or sanitize — almost every word they uttered. I knew I deserved better and could manage more.

Second, I remembered, as a professional adult, recognizing that clients would respond more positively to the truth, even if it was less then favorable. I also noticed that brands represented truthfully were more successful than those that practiced aspirational marketing (a euphemism for fake it till you make it). Astute as I am, I began to sense a correlation. (And people say I'm slow?)

All adults were children. Children long for truth. Therefore, all adults must long for truth. A + B = C.

After that epiphany, my anxiety subsided. I realized all I had to do, regardless of the number of children assembled, was tell the truth. And since children have infallible BS meters — and haven't yet adopted all the fears and trepidations of adults — they had an even easier time accepting the truth than I had telling it.

Then I knew: As children go, so goes the world.

Tell the truth.

Martin the Marlin

The Naked Truth

The paragraph below is from an actual news item:

ZEPHYR COVE, Nev. — A 53-year-old man was arrested on suspicion of being naked near a high school on Lake Tahoe's east shore ... after three Whittell High School students reported spotting him tied to a rock and lying face down behind the school. When the students asked if he needed to be untied, the man answered no. Douglas County sheriff's deputies said the man told them he was watching some buzzards flying overhead at the time. The man, who said he was a freelance writer, was arrested on a charge of loitering on school grounds.

I'm one of those apparently rare people who could not be suspected of being naked. I'm either clothed, or I'm not. Maybe that's why I think the story above demands a healthy skepticism and a full measure of compassion.

At the outset, there's a discrepancy between the grounds for the man's arrest — suspicion of being naked — and the fact that three students said he was, indeed, naked. So, the dude either was suspected of being naked, or he was naked.

Which is it? How difficult could it have been to tell? I'm not saying my own experience is a necessary barometer here; but every time I've been suspected of being naked, I've been naked.

Then there are the circumstances under which the poor guy was found. This is exactly why I'm no longer naked — ever — when I tie myself to a rock. I don't know precisely when the act came to be so profoundly misunderstood by so many. But you'll just have to trust me: this is a practice as innocuous as the day is long.

I used to tie myself to rocks in all manner of public places — school yards, parks, street corners — and no one would bat an eye, let alone call the police. I once tied myself to the Tucson Meteorite in the Smithsonian. I'd only meant to be there for a few hours, but the security guards brought me coffee and donuts for three days. We actually grew quite close. Alas, those days are gone.

Another thing: I don't know how many hardcore buzzard-watchers there are out there. But all of us who practice the art can tell you it's a source of dizziness like no other. One need not tie oneself to a rock to maintain balance; however, studies have shown that doing so significantly reduces the incidence of teetering, stumbling, and falling that can result from staring straight up for hours on end, watching the big birds reel and swoop.

And much will be made of the fact that the man was discovered facedown. That's to be expected from a population of media-hacks and law-enforcement personnel largely comprising avowed non-buzzard-watchers. Among ornithological specialists, buzzards are notorious for their shyness. Buzzards will go into hiding for weeks, going without food or bio-breaks, if they even suspect someone might be looking.

The trick is to pretend you're actually watching worms. Then, when you hear the flutter of wings and the whoosh of the bird overhead, you turn your head slowly and carefully, opening just the exposed eye ever so slightly. The difficulty of this practice is offset by the fact that buzzards also happen to be extremely gullible. They not only fall for the worm-watching trick every time, but they also love to listen to politicians and to have quarters pulled from behind their ears.

I have several large rocks in my yard, each of which provides an opportunity to lash myself to it, without fear of reprisal, retribution, or incarceration. But even there — in the privacy of my own little piece of the planet — I no longer engage in the practice au naturel. It's simply not worth the risk that the mailman or old Mrs. Anderson from next door might show up, leaving me to end the day in shame, handcuffs, and an orange jumpsuit.

The buzzards stopped coming by once I stepped down from public office and ran out of quarters. But I'm learning to adjust.

As our unfortunate friend from Zephyr Cove now knows, it's harder to live in the world once you know the naked truth.

licensed from clipartof.com

Meeting My Match

In case you missed it, the Wall Street Journal reported in late September of 2019 that the FTC was suing Match.com for:

... allegedly using fake love-interest advertisements to trick hundreds of thousands of users into buying subscriptions.

This is the rough equivalent of reporting that the Vatican is suing Pope Francis for being Catholic. What the hell did anyone expect? If you make money by selling subscriptions, you sell subscriptions, no matter what you have to do to sell them. And from what I can recall, I don't believe the word, "scrupulous", appears in any of the contractual language Match.com uses with any of its hornswoggled customers. Caveat emptor, indeed.

Part One: Bless Me, Father, For I Have ...

Yes. I confess it. Before I was fortunate enough to meet my lovely wife (thank you, God!), I was on a dating site. Okay. I was on two dating sites. The first one was Match.com. That's where I started to learn the online-dating ropes.

I won't go into all the details here. Suffice it to say, online dating sites have a peculiar code. Nothing can be taken at face value. And you have to endure a few disasters before you start to understand that this (whatever "this" might be) actually means that (and "that" is initially unexpected and always disarmingly unpleasant).

While I never posted it, my experience on Match.com inspired me to compose the ultimate dating-site profile. I offer it here as a public service and grant universal permission to use it, with two caveats:

1. Do NOT give me a footnote.

2. Make sure you've wiped it clean of my fingerprints.

Here it is:

After swimming in the lake and digging for clams on the sandbars at high tide, I love to have a fire in the fireplace on the beach while I snuggle up with that special someone during a thunderstorm to hold hands and watch a romantic movie or the Red Sox as the first snow flies and cherry blossoms bloom from beneath the autumn leaves while the Giants beat the Celtics with a good book and my cats run through the bright sunshine toward the paddock where I keep my horse next to the shed in which my canoe waits for morning paddles following Bikram yogalates and re-reading The Power of Now on my bike with my dog panting behind me and my canary silhouetted against the full moon in an inky sky brilliant with starlight and a glass of wine accompanied by smooth, classic country jazz/rock symphonies on my iPod, on which I'm running a planning app to regiment to the nth degree my next spontaneous weekend getaway to cross-country ski Antarctica after snorkeling in the BVI and going into the City for coffee and/or a show on the way to Florence or Paris for gourmet food and having good friends come over.

That captures all of the rapturous bullshit people routinely fall for on dating sites. The only thing you'll need besides that profile is the appropriate fake photo, the obtaining of which is now easier than ever, thanks to websites that auto-generate headshots using artificial intelligence.

During my brief tenure on Match.com, I was guilty of (being accused of anything on a dating site is the legal equivalent of being guilty) (1) misleading a woman I'd never met, who was looking for a surrogate for the son she'd just sent off to college, into thinking we were already married (I didn't and we weren't); (2) stalking a woman who'd posted photos of herself in her underwear, posing in her bathroom (I didn't and didn't want to); and (3) stealing the identity of a fictional character in an alleged attempt to get into a movie that was being produced about that fictional character (in hindsight, I actually wish I'd done that one).

My short Match.com experience came to a none-too-soon end after the one and only date I ever arranged through the site. I invited a woman to join me for dinner and a theater performance. During dinner, I asked her how long she'd been on Match.com. She told me nine years.

"That's a long time," I said. "What do you want?"

"I don't know," she replied. "But I know what I don't want."

"Check, please!"

Part Two: New Meanings

The second dating site I was on, which I joined when I was older but demonstrably none the wiser, was OurTime.com. (Yes. I also confess I'm a glutton for punishment.) In case you're curious, there are two distinct differences between Match.com and OurTime.com:

First, unlike Match.com, which has no age criteria, OurTime.com is a site for people over 50. The good news is if you're over 50 and looking for someone in your chronological neighborhood, you might find someone, factoring in the heavy odds against success with online dating, of course. The bad news is there's no limit to the over 50 part. So, you may very well find a dating candidate older than your mom, who's looking for that special someone to take her out of the home on weekends.

Second, on OurTime.com, no means yes and vice versa. That means you're likely to hear from people you contact in inverse proportion to the rudeness with which they rebuff your initial overtures — or you'll never hear another peep from those who seem most enthusiastic at first blush. Go figure.

My experience on OurTime.com hit closer to my heart than did my experience on Match.com — but only if I carried my wallet in my left breast pocket. At the end of the relationship with the one and only woman I consented to meet from my sojourn on OurTime.com, my bank balance was almost as low as my self-esteem and my IQ.

I later met other people who'd interacted with the woman I met on OurTime.com. Those people said things about her like, "I'd never met a real con artist before meeting her," and "She has no conscience." I'm sure you know people like the ones who made those comments. They're the ones who, if you're too stupid to figure it out for yourself (guilty), won't tell you you're being fleeced while you're being fleeced. But they'll line up to tell you you've been sheared to the skin after you've been sheared to the skin. But all was not lost ...

Part Three: Luck O' the Irish

In March of 2000, I'd gone to work at an ad agency. There were two (and only two) people in the agency who were bulletproof — so talented they'd never be fired. One was the Creative Director. His name was Dan. (Still is, I'd imagine; although, we're no longer in touch.) The other was a copywriter. Her name is Judy. (Still is, I'm sure, because we're still in touch.)

I left the agency in 2004. (See " I Volunteered for This".) Judy left before I did. But we maintained our contact over the ensuing years. During the entire time I was quixotically and masochistically enduring my online-dating travails, Judy would be saying, "You really need to meet my friend, Anne." Because I'm an idiot, I'd routinely reply, "No. I don't think so." At the same time, Judy would be calling Anne and saying, "You really need to meet my friend, Mark." Because Anne's extremely intelligent and a very good judge of character, she'd routinely reply, "No. I don't think so." And so it went, until ...

My OurTime.com debacle ended in January of 2015. I was despondent, horrified by my own stupidity, and quite unable to process the extent to which I'd let myself be taken advantage of. Judy called again. Again, I begged off. I told her about the disaster and my staggering naïveté. I told her I needed some time to lick my wounds.

Judy called again in late March. She explained to me that she's the Queen of Rationalization (she is). She told me she could find the silver lining in a septic tank (she can). I thanked her and told her I'd let her know when I felt a little more steady.

In a conversation shortly thereafter with my friend, Chuck, I shared all of that — the OurTime.com fiasco, the calls from Judy, my reluctance to come out from under my bed or to expose myself to sunlight, my reticence to meet Anne. He told me I was taking everything way too seriously. He suggested I look at the opportunity to meet Anne as an adventure, as a way to get out of the house, out of my head, and to enjoy some simple social interaction. In April of 2015, I decided Chuck was right. I called Judy. Then I called Anne.

We agreed to meet on Saturday, April 18, at noon, at R.J. Julia Booksellers in Madison, Connecticut. I told Anne I was fairly certain I knew what I looked like but was a little less certain I'd be able to recognize her. She said, "I'll be the one in the leopard shoes." And sure enough: As I sat on the bench in front of the bookstore that day, apprehensively, I saw a beautiful woman approaching from my left.

She wore blue jeans, a blue Oxford shirt, a tasteful blazer, and leopard flats. She walked as if she didn't have a care in the world. She smiled as if she knew the world smiled back. Her eyes shone from within. And they were completely clear — no guile, no avarice, no artifice, no pretense, no expectation — radiating only innocent joy and a very contagious peace.

After chatting our way through R.J. Julia, we carried the conversation across the Connecticut River from Madison to Niantic. We had lunch in the village, after which we went to the Book Barn. (The four words you never say in the Book Barn are, "It's time to leave.") We continued the conversation back across the river to Westbrook (where I lived at the time) to sit on the beach and talk some more. Then we went back to Madison, sat in an ice cream shop for a while, and jabbered on as if we'd known each other for years. We parted company at 9:30, thus ending our nine-and-a-half hour first date.

On Anne's birthday in July of 2016, I asked her to marry me. In a monumental lapse of her otherwise unerring judgment of character, she said yes. We were married on the 11th day of the sixth month of 2017 (because I wanted to be a June bride). Anne's cousin, Tom, the pastor at a local church, performed the ceremony. I wore Anne's late father's tie. Judy gave the toast at our reception.

Part Four: New Beginnings

From September of 1979 to January of 1982 (when I finally woke up and went to college), I worked in an appliance-distribution warehouse. I spent my days unloading trailers full of TVs, console stereos (remember those?), refrigerators, dishwashers, microwave ovens, and more. I was lost, directionless, unsure of myself, and less sure of my future.

One day, a gentleman named Ernie Santoro from the Sales Department — a big, garrulous fellow with a walrus mustache — came walking through the warehouse. Without breaking stride, without taking his eyes off me, and all the while keeping his left index finger pointed at me, he said: "O'Brien, you lead a charmed life." I thought, "I have no idea what you're talking about, Ernie. In all likelihood, neither do you."

But he was right.

Some people take longer to bloom than others. I'm one of them. I've always known it. I've come to a comfortable co-existence with the knowledge.

I told Anne two things when I came to know her well. First, I said, "I haven't met my match. I've met my equal." Then I said, "It didn't take me 60 years to find you. It took me 60 years to be able to recognize you when I did."

The woman is like the tide: she comes and goes.
She knows the things that I can just suppose.
(Dan Fogelberg, from the song, "Comes and Goes")

Charmed life, indeed.

©Mark Nelson O'Brien